STONEWALLED

MYSTERY HISTORY
- BOOK THREE -

By Sonny Barber

Historic references are intended to be as accurate as possible, with the exception of some actual persons whose activities and events have been dramatized. In the present-day part of the book, names, characters, businesses, places, events, and incidents are products of the author's imagination and are used in a fictitious manner. Any resemblance to actual persons, living or dead, or actual events is purely coincidental.

Cover design by AuthorSupport.com
ISBN: 1519351291
ISBN 13: 9781519351296
Library of Congress Control Number: 2015919392
CreateSpace Independent Publishing Platform
North Charleston, South Carolina

To the many teachers who instilled in me a love of American history, and to all those who, today, teach and preserve that history. And to my wife, Barbara, who remains my most ardent supporter and forthright critic.

Acknowledgments

My thanks again to my wife, Barbara, a Rhode Island native, who first took me to Little Compton many years ago and convinced me that we should spend as much time as possible in this precious gem by the sea.

The inspiration for this book came from my good friend, our summer landlord at Downwind Farm, gifted illustrator, and phenomenal bass player, Gail Greenwood. A lifelong resident of Rhode Island, Gail's always fighting against unbridled development in urban, suburban and rural areas of her home state. Her friendship and that of her long-time companion, Chil, and their "children," Bear Bear and Maurice, make our summers in Little Compton seem like coming home.

Thanks also to the Little Compton Historical Society and its special exhibition publication, *Portraits in Time, Three Centuries of Remarkable Residents 1600–1900.*

The Mystery History Series
www.sonnybarber.com

Book One—*Crossed and Found*

Book Two—*Gold Hush*

Book Three—*Stonewalled*

Available at Amazon.com in paperback and Kindle

Stonewalled:
delayed, obstructed, or prevented from doing something

CHAPTER ONE

Summer 1675, near the Sakonnet River, Plymouth Colony

Sassamon ran across the open field toward the tree line, his pounding heart keeping time with the thud of his moccasins slamming against the ground.

Another Sakonnet tribesman, whom everyone called "Honest George," ran alongside him and called out, "Stop! I must rest."

"We can't. They'll catch us, and we'll be in range of their muskets."

More than half an hour had passed since two of Chief Metacomet's Wampanoag warriors had spotted Sassamon and George and chased them across the countryside. Safety for the men was half a mile away at the Sakonnets' summer encampment, located on a low hill with views of the wide river. A thick forest of white pine, maple, and oak trees shaded the summer home for the men and women of the tribe. Season after season, they fished in the river, dug clams in the shallows, and tended plots of corn.

A sharp stone punctured Sassamon's left moccasin. He winced and stumbled to the ground, dropping his musket.

George reached down and pulled his friend up.

With pain shooting up his leg, Sassamon took three hobbled steps. He caught sight of the warriors behind him. "Go! I'll meet up with you."

George ran ahead and scrambled behind a large tree.

"Load your musket," Sassamon said, limping to a tree next to his friend.

The men sat, backs against the trees, muskets across their laps, and fingers on the triggers.

George peeked around the tree and jerked his head back. "I hear them."

His knees twitching back and forth, Sassamon raised his hand, palm open. "Wait."

The muffled sound of moccasin-clad feet thrashing through the high grass grew louder.

Twisting around and laying on the ground, the Sakonnet tribesmen faced their attackers. Sassamon squeezed the trigger. The flash from the musket blast sent the Wampanoag warriors leaping to the side to avoid the lead ball whizzing past them.

George yanked the trigger of his musket, but there was no loud bang, and no black smoke coming from the barrel.

Sassamon's eyes were as big as the clams he dug from the river.

The Wampanoags dropped their muskets and ran toward the men, waving their hatchets in the air and screaming.

With his musket reloaded, Sassamon whirled around from the protection of the tree and yanked the trigger.

One of the warriors yelped, grabbed his leg, and plowed into the ground, shoulder first. His companion ran back and pulled the man up. Wrapping the man's arm around his neck, the companion picked up both muskets, ran a few steps in the other direction, and settled into a fast walk.

"We must go quickly," Sassamon said. "Darkness is upon us."

The two broke into a jog, heading for the Sakonnet camp.

Breathing hard, the messengers ran into the crowd gathered around a large fire.

Awashonks, the sachem or chief of the tribe, twisted and gyrated in a frenzied dance around the blazing pile of pine boughs and twigs. Perspiration dripping from her forehead, she tilted her head at the sky and chanted, her voice echoing through the forest. Other members of the tribe joined in the ritual dance, following her around the ring of stones and the crackling and sizzling fire. The sachem stopped and raised her arms, her voice trailing off into whispered words and then becoming quiet. She motioned to the two men to join her. "Where is Benjamin Church?"

"He was not at his house." Sassamon looked back at George. "I don't believe anyone has been there for many days. Two Wampanoag warriors chased us after we left his house. I wounded one, and they ran away."

"Metacomet sent men to ask me to join him in fighting the English," Awashonks said. "Church promised he would tell the English in Plymouth that we would join him if the English would protect us from Metacomet."

His legs aching, Sassamon knelt on one knee. "What if the English attack *us*?"

"We will not let that happen. We also cannot join Metacomet. He has sworn to kill the English."

The sachem motioned for her council to come close. "Our peaceful place here is no more. We must prepare to abandon our home." She raised her arms, palms up, and waved them from side to side. "The Sakonnets have lived on these lands for many seasons—long before the white man came. We marked this land as our own. Others who come will know this is the land of the Sakonnet." With the last rays of the setting sun lighting the sky in bright, yellow streaks, her voice trailed off into a loud whisper. "We must leave. War is coming."

CHAPTER TWO

Present day, Little Compton, Rhode Island

Kay Telfair backed up to the three-foot-high wall of neatly placed stones and hoisted herself up. The fourteen-year-old twisted to see behind her and pointed across the open field toward the Sakonnet River. "What are those men doing over there? One has a telescope. He's aiming it at that other man with the stick."

"That's not a telescope," Bobbie, her mom, said. "It's called a 'transit.' That's the thing your grandfather used when he surveyed land."

"Why would they be surveying?"

Kay's mom repositioned her coffee mug on the rough surface of the wall and reached down and tied the laces on her sneaker. "I'm not sure. Maybe somebody's going to build something." She stood, waving her left hand and lifting the mug. "What a view—the land running down to the water's edge, the blue sky, and the puffy clouds. It doesn't get much better than this."

"I have to admit this is pretty nice." The young teen wiggled onto a smoother spot and tapped the stone next to her. "I wonder who built these walls. It must've taken somebody a long time to pile these up and make them perfectly straight and even on top."

"We can take a trip to the historical society on a rainy day and find out. That'll give us something to do besides going to the beach and shopping at the farm markets."

"That'll be fun." Kay gave her mom her classic eye-roll.

"Don't tell me you've lost that Kay Telfair burning curiosity."

"Yes, I would like to know who built the walls. But, Mom, there's nothing to do here in Little Compton. Why didn't we stay in Newport?"

"We could've stayed there, and it would have been much easier on your father. He has to drive fifty miles round trip to the Navy War College for the next two weeks. But we decided a quiet time away from all the tourists would make this a better vacation."

"*We're* tourists. We live in New Jersey, remember?"

"You know what I mean—away from crowds and traffic. And besides, we're not exactly tourists. I was born in Rhode Island and I went to school here. And your dad and I met in Newport when he was in Officer Candidate School."

Kay took in a deep breath and gave the "I'm bored" sigh. "OK. We're not tourists, but I don't see why we couldn't stay in a place with a little more going on. We were away from tourists last year in Maine. Why couldn't we have a change this summer?"

"Kay, it's done. We're here." Bobbie paused. "Speaking of Maine, have you heard from Matt Hubbard since he called you at Christmas?"

"He texted me a few times, but it was mostly about the weather and lobsters."

"Didn't you say he had an aunt in Rhode Island?"

"Yes. She lives in Tiverton."

"Does he know you're in Rhode Island?"

"I did mention in a text that we'd be staying at Windcrest Farm this month, and I sent him the address. He said he hoped I had a great time."

"Nothing about seeing you?"

"No. Nothing."

A cool breeze blew across the pasture with a horse grazing in the distant corner. Kay stared down the long hill toward the river. The shadow of a cloud moved across the water, changing its color from a bluish green to gray and back again.

"I wish Anna were here now," Kay said.

"We wanted her to ride up with us, but she had signed up for soccer camp by the time we booked the house. She'll be here in a few days." Bobbie took a swig from her mug. "Coffee's cold. Let's go back to the house."

"Hi, ladies," came a woman's voice from behind them.

Kay's mom whipped around, sloshing her cold coffee over the rim of her mug.

The young woman extended her hand. "I'm Elena Clifford. Sorry I wasn't here to greet you when you arrived. I had to take my husband..." She cleared her throat. "What I mean is, we were away for a couple of days."

"Pleased to finally meet you in person. I'm Bobbie, and this is my daughter, Kay."

Reaching out to shake Elena's hand, Kay focused on the woman's eyes, which showed the dark circles of someone who was severely sleep-deprived.

"I saw you and Kay walking. Is there anything you need at the house?"

"No. It's perfect. We love the house. Don't we, Kay."

"Yes, we do. It's very nice...and quiet. Almost too quiet."

Bobbie glared at her daughter.

"What I mean is, it's very relaxing being here," Kay said. "And I love your flower garden."

"I might have overdone it with the flowers, but people keep stopping at the stand and buying them."

"They *are* beautiful," Bobbie said. "How do you collect the money?"

"I do it on the honor system. They can make a bouquet that fits in one of the jars, and then drop the money in the box."

Kay hopped off the wall and brushed the back of her capris. "Who built these walls? They're everywhere in Little Compton."

"The farmers found the stones when they plowed and moved them to the edge of the fields," Elena said. "The piles were later made into these walls, which served as fencing. Some were built by the Native Americans. The settlers got them to make these walls to pay back debts for things they bought from the English. Most of these were built in the late eighteenth and early nineteenth century."

Kay rubbed a flat stone that formed part of the top of the long wall. "There must be hundreds of miles of these things here."

Elena nodded, eyeing the line of skillfully stacked granite and slate. "A popular story around here says that, in the early 1700s, a man named Thomas Church bragged to his colleagues in the colonial legislature that there were enough stone walls to reach all the way from Little Compton to Boston. That's about seventy-five miles. They didn't believe him, so he went home to check his facts. At the next session of the legislature, he told them that he'd been wrong. He said there were enough stone walls to reach from Little Compton to Boston and *back again*. A professor at the University of Connecticut did a study and estimates that there are enough stone walls in all of New England to reach to the moon."

"I'm surprised the walls didn't get torn down over the years," Bobbie said.

"That surprises a lot of people. I read somewhere that the land was too rocky for large-scale farming, and there was no reason to tear down the walls." Elena stared at the surveyors. "There was another reason, at least until a couple of years ago. Little Compton's a bit off the beaten track, and that used to discourage developers."

"I can see why people would want to move here," Bobbie said. "You have the beautiful farmland, the stone walls, and the ocean. It's breathtaking. And the view from here down to the river is spectacular."

"Yes, it is a great view," Elena said. "For a little while longer, anyway." She pointed toward the river. "Someone bought the land, and they're going to build some big houses over there."

"I thought Windcrest Farm went all the way to the river?" Bobbie said.

"The original farm did include the land down to the Sakonnet. I don't know when that parcel of land was sold. We bought Windcrest as it is now."

Bobbie forgot about her cold coffee and brought the mug to her lips. "Ugh. I could use a fresh cup. Elena, would you like some coffee? We haven't had our second round of caffeine yet."

"I...I...yeah, sure. That would be great. Haven't had any yet. Busy morning."

Kay's mom led the way across the field to the larger rental house, which stood about seventy-five feet from Elena's small cottage.

Walking onto the porch, Kay laid the tray of coffee mugs on the table and pulled up a chair next to Elena. "This house is bigger than the one you're living in. Why don't you live here, and rent out the smaller one?"

"Kay, that's a bit personal," her mom said, stepping onto the porch with the carafe of coffee.

"Sorry, but I was—"

"It's a logical question." Elena gave a weak smile, glanced at her watch, and looked toward the cottage. "This house rents for more, and you can sleep six people using the sofa bed. Zack and I make more money in the summer season this way than if we rented the cottage. There're only two of us, and we don't need much space. The cottage is on one level, like this house, and that makes it...anyway, it works for me and Zack."

"Ah, nectar of the gods," Bobbie said, caressing her mug and taking a sip. "How long have you and your husband lived in Little Compton?"

"Two years, but we bought the property six years ago. We moved here after Zack was...after he got out of the navy. We took on a mortgage, but the rent from the house means I don't have to work full time. That way Zack...anyway, it works out."

"You said Zack was in the navy. My husband, Jim, was in the navy for four years, and he's now in the reserves. He's doing his two weeks of active duty at the Navy War College."

"This is quite a place to maintain," Kay said. "It must keep you and your husband pretty busy."

"I...that is, *we*...Zack and I manage to keep it together."

For the next fifteen minutes, the three women talked about the variety of flowers in Elena's garden, the chances of rain that day, and recommendations on places to eat in the area.

"I've taken up enough of your vacation time," Elena said. "I should be going. I have to teach a class at the high school later this morning, and I need to run a few errands for Zack."

"I started high school last year." Kay tucked her light brown hair over her ears.

Elena raised her eyebrows at Kay. "You've only finished your first year? I thought you were a junior or senior."

"I'm fourteen, going on fifteen—in three months. When you're five-foot-seven, people think you're older. How old are you?"

Bobbie gasped. "Kay, women don't ask other women about their age."

"I'm not offended. I'm twenty-nine, but I wish I had the energy of a teen these days."

"What do you teach?" Kay asked.

"I teach music part time in the summer, and I help the bandmaster at the high school during the school year."

Kay's mom wrapped her hands around her mug. "And what does your husband do?"

"He…he works out of the house." Elena grasped her watch, rotating the band until the face centered on the top of her wrist. "Zack does things on the computer." She stared at her watch once more. "I've got to get going. Thanks for the coffee."

Elena walked ahead of Bobbie to the front door. "Let me know if you need anything."

"We will," Bobbie said.

Kay gathered the coffee mugs, placed them in the sink, and peered out the kitchen window at the cottage. "'Does things on the computer? I wonder what that means?"

Bobbie walked up beside her daughter. "What's the mystery? His work involves using a computer. Some people are very private."

Kay drew back from the window. "I understand that, but why didn't she want to tell us? There're a hundred things people do on the computer."

"Knowing you, you'll have all the details by the time we leave here."

"Thanks a lot, Mom. I'm not like that."

Bobbie gave Kay the classic motherly, patronizing peck on the cheek. "Of course you aren't, dear."

"Maybe I am." Kay grinned and touched her mom's head with her own. "But that makes me special, right?"

"That you are," Bobbie said, chuckling and shaking her head. "Definitely one of a kind."

CHAPTER THREE

The rain pinged on the metal roof of the screened porch, filled the gutters, and gushed from the downspouts.

"I'm glad we went for our walk early," Bobbie said. "Don't you love the sound of the rain?"

Kay kept her attention on the phone screen. "What? Sure. Yeah, the sound of the rain."

"It makes me sleepy. But I don't want to take a nap. I won't be able to sleep tonight." Bobbie yawned and covered her mouth with the back of her hand. "The bad thing about this rain is that your dad will have to drive in it from Newport this evening."

Kay typed the last letters of a text.

"Speaking of Dad, I thought he was going to have time to spend with us during his navy reserve duty."

"That was the plan. But he's been asked to help with some super-secret project that has a short deadline. He can't tell us what it is."

"I understand that," Kay said, "but he's leaving before I get up in the morning, and he got home last night at nine. He's here for two weeks, and then he has to go back to work. I wish he could stay for the whole time we're here."

"I'm as disappointed as you." Bobbie shook her head. "Let's change the subject. Did you hear from Anna?"

"Yes. She said she's coming up on the train tomorrow afternoon. I told her we'd pick her up at the station in Providence. I wish she could have driven up with us last Saturday. It's a little boring around here."

Bobbie sat up in the chaise and faked a frown. "You don't like spending time with me, your beloved mother?"

"No, no. I don't mean I'm bored with you. It's just that …well… you're my mom. I love you, but—"

"I'm kidding. How about reading the book you downloaded."

"I can't get into it for some reason."

"There're some books on Little Compton and Rhode Island history on the bookshelf in the living room. You like history."

"*That* should put me right to sleep." Kay took in a deep breath and slouched in her chair.

"We can't go to the beach," Bobbie said. "It's raining harder." She scanned her phone. "And the weather report says we'll have rain for a few hours." Bobbie left the porch, returned with three books, and stacked them on the table next to her daughter. "I'm going to find something for lunch."

• • •

Bobbie slid a plate in front of Kay. "Lunch is served."

"Thanks," Kay said, glancing at her mom and then staring at a page in the book. "Did you know that Little Compton used to be part of Massachusetts? It was part of the Plymouth Colony. That's where the Pilgrims landed on the *Mayflower*—at Plymouth."

"We went to see Plymouth Rock and the Plantation when you were about seven. Do you remember that?"

"Yep, I do. We also went to see the *Mayflower*. It was a replica of the first one, if I remember correctly." Kay spread open the pages of her book. "The Pilgrims were supposed to settle somewhere between Chesapeake Bay and the Hudson River in New York—before it was New York. But, a storm blew them off course, and they wound up in Massachusetts."

"I did not know that," Bobbie said. "Or maybe I forgot. It's been quite a while since I took a history class."

Kay flipped through more pages between bites. "There was a Native American tribe called the Sakonnets who lived here. That must be how the river got its name. They were part of the Wampanoags, who were another tribe, and they lived all over this area." She turned a page. "Interesting. It says that in the 1600s, a woman was the head of the Sakonnet tribe; she was called a sachem. This book says she was friends with Benjamin Church, who was the first settler in Little Compton."

Kay's mom stuffed a lettuce leaf back into her sandwich. "Was that the name of the guy Elena mentioned in her story about the stone walls stretching to Boston?"

"I think she said Timothy Church, or Thomas, or something like that." Kay scanned her book's index and turned some pages. "It was Thomas Church. He was Benjamin's son."

"That's all very interesting," Bobbie said. "But, can you please stop reading for one minute and eat."

Kay held the sandwich with one hand, took a bite, and, ignoring her mother, spread the pages of the book open with the other hand. "Here's something…" She garbled the last few words.

"I forgot my vitamins," Bobbie said. "And please don't talk with food in your mouth."

Knock, knock.

"Would you see who's at the door, please," Bobbie said, walking toward the bedroom.

Lost in her research, Kay flipped a page in the book.

"Hello?" A man's voice boomed through the screen door. "Anyone at home?"

"Mom, somebody's at the door."

"I know. See who it is, please."

Kay laid the book facedown to hold her place and walked to the front door. A six-foot-tall man with a well-trimmed beard and an orange ball cap stood on the porch.

"Can I help you?"

"Hi. My name's Henry McCallum." The man pointed toward the river. "We're building houses down there, and we're finishing up the excavation for a basement. Our equipment might be making some noise tomorrow. The crew is going to start early, around seven thirty. I wanted to—"

Bobbie walked up in front of her daughter. "What is it you wanted?"

"I was saying that we'll be making some noise with our equipment for a few hours tomorrow. I'm apologizing in advance."

"Do the Cliffords know you're doing this?" Bobbie pointed at the cottage. "We're renting this house from them for a few weeks."

"Yes. I know Mrs. Clifford rents this house in the summer and lives in the cottage. I didn't speak to her. I left her a note. I...well...we don't see eye-to-eye on some things." The man cleared his throat. "I wanted you to know the noise might be loud."

"Why do you want to block Elena's view of the river?"

Bobbie tugged on her daughter's arm. "Kay."

The man looked at Kay, his lips beginning to outline a smile that never quite made it, and then turned to Bobbie. "I understand. I'm not the most popular person in town these days. But I try not to worry too much. This is my job."

Kay stared at McCallum. "But you're destroying the farmland and the view."

"That's enough, Kay."

"Sorry to bother you," McCallum said, a smile barely breaking the corners of his mouth. He went to his truck, closed the door, and poked his head out the window. "I'm really sorry to have to disturb you. I promise; we'll be done by tomorrow afternoon."

Kay backed into the house.

Her mom closed the door. "You were a bit rude to that man."

"I'm sorry. I couldn't help myself."

"I know you're sympathetic to Elena's situation, but think about what you're saying—before you say it."

"OK, I'll try. I mean, I will." Kay sat, opened her book, and looked up at her mom. "I don't think that man, McCallum, likes his job."

"What makes you think that?"

"I'm not sure. He just gives me that impression."

CHAPTER FOUR

"**S**ounds like another one of the trucks," Kay said. "How many do they need? The man said yesterday they'd be done digging today."

Bobbie walked to the window. "It's a red pickup, and it's stopped next to our van. But it's not from the construction company."

"Hi, Matt." Bobbie opened the door for seventeen-year-old Matt Hubbard of Prospect Harbor, Maine. "Kay, guess who's here."

Kay brushed past her mom. Should she be surprised or a little angry? He hadn't communicated that much with her. "You didn't tell me you were coming to Rhode Island."

"I didn't know myself until a few days ago."

"Come in," Bobbie said. "Have you had lunch?"

"No, ma'am, sure haven't. I was running errands for my aunt and thought I'd stop by."

"I'll make you a sandwich."

"Thanks, Mrs. Telfair, but I—."

"Sit, please." Bobbie gripped Matt's arm and led him to the table on the porch.

Kay sat across the table from him. "Why *are* you here?"

Matt chuckled. "It's nice to see you, too, Kay."

Kay's face warmed, but it wasn't full-blown blushing. "I'm sorry. I was surprised. I haven't talked to you in a long time. I was wondering why you were here in Rhode Island?"

"You did text me and tell me you were going to be here at the farm. You *are* glad to see me, aren't you?"

"What? Yes, of course. It's just that I didn't expect you."

Bobbie glanced at her daughter. "What Kay really means is that she's glad to have someone other than me to talk to."

Kay's mouth fell open. "Mom, you make me sound like an ungrateful child."

"You know what I mean, dear. Having someone near your own age to be around." Bobbie looked at Matt. "Where are you staying?"

"My aunt and uncle in Tiverton are letting me stay with them. And talking about being around people your own age, it's like a circus being in a house with four kids. The oldest is eight."

"That should keep you busy." Bobbie slid a plate in front of Matt. "Is your dad here, too?"

"No. He's in Colorado."

In the middle of taking a bite of her sandwich, Kay covered her mouth and swallowed. "Colorado. Why?"

"He left his job in Portland and went with a company that manages forests across the country. They wanted him for a special project a few months over the summer, and I didn't want to go."

"You didn't want to go to Colorado? I love traveling out West. Mom and Dad took me to the Grand Canyon a few years ago."

"I'd planned to check out some colleges this summer and I figured I'd start in Rhode Island while my dad was away. Plus my aunt and uncle said I could stay with them."

Matt swallowed the last bite of the sandwich and looked over at Kay. "There's also another reason I didn't want to go to Colorado."

Kay set her glass on the coaster. "What's that?"

Matt's cheeks glowed. He looked at Bobbie, then down at his plate, and finally at Kay. "You told me you were coming to Little Compton this summer, and I thought there was a chance I might get to see you." He took a sip of water. "And here I am."

Startled by Matt's openness, the blood again rushed to Kay's face. No way she could hide this blushing. She glanced at her mom.

Bobbie winked at her. "That's very nice of you, Matt. Would you like another sandwich? How about you, Kay?"

"No, thanks, Mrs. Telfair. I'd better be going. I didn't mean to interrupt your day by dropping in like this."

"You didn't interrupt anything. Did he, Kay."

"Not at all." Kay put on her Christmas-morning smile—the one she showed when she got that unexpected gift. "I'm glad you came."

"Kay and I are going to pick up Anna at the train station today. She's arriving at two thirty-five," Bobbie said. "Do you want to ride with us?"

"How about Kay and I go in my truck and pick her up?"

"What do you think, Mom?"

"I guess that would be OK. Are you allowed to drive teenagers?"

"Yes, ma'am. I turned seventeen in the spring, and I have a regular license."

Bobbie nodded. "Be careful. Driving in downtown Providence can be a bit hairy."

"This will be great," Kay said. "I know Anna will be glad to see you."

"We're *all* glad to see you," Bobbie said.

Matt smiled and rotated the ball cap in his hands.

"I'll grab my wallet." Kay jogged to the bedroom, grinning from ear to ear.

CHAPTER FIVE

K ay pointed at the exit. "There she is."
Anna Gardino waved and stepped off the escalator, maneuvering her rolling duffel around other passengers.

Matt reached for the duffel. "Let me get that for you."

Anna pulled her bag close, her eyes wide, and gripped the handle with both hands. "I didn't recognize you, Matt. It's been a long time. What're you doing here?"

"Whoa. That's the second time I've gotten that greeting today."

Anna winced. "That didn't come out the way I wanted."

Kay grabbed Anna by the arm. "We'll tell you why he's here when we get in the truck. Let's get out of here. The rush hour traffic will start soon."

• • •

"That's why I'm here for the summer," Matt said. "Unless my nieces and nephews drive me crazy. Don't get me wrong. I love them, but they demand a lot of my attention. And I don't have much privacy at my aunt's. They think of me as a big brother and want to spend a lot of time with me."

"It's good practice for being a dad someday," Anna said.

"Practice? It's almost like the real thing. My four-year-old niece wants me to take her to the potty. Plus, I drove them to get ice cream when I first arrived. I was nervous having the four of them in my aunt's minivan. And then at the store it was like trying to corral lobsters."

"That's hilarious," Anna said. "Reminds me of taking care of my little brother, Buddy, when he was a toddler. What a pain."

Kay giggled. "I would love to have seen you with those little kids in the van."

"It's not so funny when you have to clean up melted ice cream off the seats. What a mess!" Matt half-smiled. "I guess it is a little funny. The kids liked it so much, they want me to take them every day now. My aunt loves it. I guess with me around, she gets some time to herself."

Anna chuckled and leaned forward on the console between the front seats. "Looks like a very busy summer, Matt. Visiting campuses, filling out applications, and going to the ice cream store with your nieces and nephews."

"Hey, this is serious!" Matt said, but in a not-so-serious tone. "This is about my future."

Anna grinned at Kay. "If college doesn't work out for you, Matt, you can always deliver ice cream for a living."

"Or become a professional babysitter." Kay tightened her lips and pressed her hand over her mouth to contain her laughter.

Anna couldn't quash hers. She burst out laughing, causing Kay to let loose with a loud cackle.

"You think this is funny, don't you." Matt pursed his lips, shot a glance at Kay, and caught a glimpse of Anna in the rearview mirror.

Anna slouched back in her seat.

Kay gazed out the passenger window. She hadn't seen Matt in almost a year, and she'd already made him angry.

Ten seconds passed with not a word uttered.

"Gotcha." Matt chuckled, glancing back and forth at the two girls. "If you saw me and those four kids piling in and out of the van with ice cream on their faces and cones dripping, I guess anybody would think it was funny."

"Trips to the ice cream store and visiting colleges can't take up all your time," Anna said. "What else do you have planned for your summer?"

"I don't know. Nothing yet."

"Hang with us." Anna, opening her eyes wide and nodding, eased her hand over the seat and tapped Kay on her right shoulder.

Kay glared at her friend and turned to Matt. "Unless you're too busy."

"Surely, Matt, you won't be too busy to be with your crew from the *Maria*," Anna said. "We were the best fishermen and divers on your lobster boat last summer." She made a fist in the air and raised her voice. "All for one and one for all."

"I don't want to mess up your summer plans," Matt said.

"You won't mess up our summer plans." Kay drew her mouth up and sneered. "We don't have any."

"That settles it," Anna said. "When you're not visiting college campuses and going to get ice cream with your nieces and nephews, you can hang with us. Right, Kay?"

"Sure. But it won't be very exciting in Little Compton—there's a reason it's not called '*Big* Compton.'"

"I wouldn't bet on things *not* being exciting," Anna said.

Kay twisted around to face her friend. "What's that supposed to mean?"

Anna tossed her head back and looked out the window. "Oh, nothing—nothing at all."

Matt checked the rearview mirror, smiling at Anna, and stole a split-second glance at Kay in the passenger's seat. "I think she means that excitement finds *you,* Kay. "

Kay faked a sad expression, her bottom lip pouting. "I want new friends. I know you both don't like me. You're out of my will."

Anna reached up front and poked her friend. "Stop it, you big baby. We like her don't we, Matt?"

"What? Yeah, sure. I...we like you. Very much."

CHAPTER SIX

"**B**ye, Matt. Thanks for the ride." Anna waved and rolled her bag inside the house.

"Anna." Bobbie hugged her daughter's best friend. "We're glad you're here."

"Let's get you settled in our room," Kay said. "And you'd better not snore."

"I don't snore."

"I'll record it on my phone next time. Believe me; you snore."

"At least I don't talk in my sleep."

"Sometimes I have very vivid dreams."

"I'll say. In Maine you said someone was chasing you in your dream and trying to hit you with a frying pan. Then another time you dreamed you fell into…let's just say you have some strange dreams."

"I know the dream you're talking about—the one where I fall off the bridge into the Delaware River. I wake up before I hit the water. I have that one a lot." Kay plucked a pair of jeans from Anna's duffel. "You can hang stuff on this side of the closet. And let's not talk about dreams anymore."

"Sure. Let's talk about you and Matt. I thought you said he had kind of forgotten you, and you had written him off."

"I didn't say that exactly. It's just that we haven't talked much this past year."

"I don't think he's forgotten you. He's thinking about going to college in Rhode Island. It's closer to New Jersey…and you."

"Will you stop with the me and Matt thing." Kay twisted around. "It's annoying." She scooped up a pillow and threw it at Anna. "You can be a pain. I don't know why I let you be my best friend."

"*Let me?* That's a laugh." Anna did a two-handed toss with the pillow, hitting Kay in the face.

"Ouch!" Kay put on a fake frown. "That's right—I *let* you be my friend."

"After all the craziness you put me through last summer, you're lucky I'm your friend at all."

Kay moved closer to Anna and held out her hand. "Fist bump. I'm glad you're here—snoring and all."

Anna instead gave her best friend a hug.

Kay gave Anna her famous light-fingered, pat-on-the-back hug.

"What a fake hug," Anna said. "You're a jerk."

"So are you."

"Am not."

"Are, too."

Kay went to the closet and slipped a pair of Anna's jeans over a hanger. "I really am glad you're here."

CHAPTER SEVEN

"I can't believe you wore that suit." Kay shifted her beach chair to get into the shade of the umbrella. "It's a bit revealing."

"What's wrong with it?" Anna fanned her hand across her body. "Just because you wore one of your one-piece swim team suits doesn't mean I can't wear what I want."

"I wore this because I'm going to do some serious swimming."

Kay's mom looked up from her e-reader. "You both look very nice."

"You could've worn your other suit," Anna said.

"Whatever."

"Please don't use that word," Kay's mom said. "It's rude."

"I'm very hurt." Anna put on a fake lip quiver and turned away, fighting back her laughter.

Kay shook her head. "Oh, stop it."

"Why don't you girls take a stroll down the beach. Pick up some shells and enjoy the beautiful day. I'll sit here and read." She took in a breath, gazed out at the ocean, and slowly exhaled. "In peace and quiet."

"Whoopee," Kay said. "When somebody asks me what I did on my summer vacation, I can say I picked up shells for a month at South Shore Beach in exciting Little Compton, Rhode Island."

"I give up." Bobbie picked up her reader. "Go for a walk, and if you don't want to pick up shells, don't."

Ten yards down the beach, Anna leaned in toward her friend. "You might want to stop bringing up how bored you are. I think you've pushed your mom to the brink."

"I guess."

"Let's go down to where those surfers are," Anna said. "Have you ever surfed?"

"Tried once when we took a trip to California. I was eleven. I didn't like it that much. I fell off the board a lot. It's a lot harder than it looks. Plus, the waves in the Pacific were huge, and the water was freezing."

"I'd like to try it someday."

"I thought you didn't like swimming."

"Sometimes I don't, but today, maybe I do."

"What-*ev-er*."

Anna shook her finger at Kay. "Naughty, naughty. Remember what your mom said."

"My mom's not standing here." Kay walked into the water and turned back to her friend. "Whatever, whatever, whatever. *There*."

"You're hopeless." Anna shook her head and followed Kay. "This water is amazing. I didn't know it would be so clear."

A young girl and an older boy paddled out through the low waves on their surfboards. The boy caught a wave, and raced to shore, followed by the girl.

"That guy's pretty good," Anna said. She turned to Kay. "I could do that."

"Believe me; it's not that easy."

The boy yelled, his board skimming toward Anna. "Look out! Coming in."

She jumped and fell backward, sitting chest-high in the cold water.

The young girl surfer came speeding in. Kay high-stepped back a few feet, avoiding the same fate as Anna.

The boy yanked on his board's leash and pulled it next to him. "Are you all right?" He reached out, grabbed Anna's hand, and pulled her up.

"I'm OK," she said, tugging at her swimsuit and brushing back her dark brown and very wet hair. "Thanks."

"My name's Hank." Lifting one end of his board, the young surfer steadied himself in the shifting sandy bottom. "What's yours?"

"Anna." She looked back toward the shore. "And that's my friend..."

"I'm right behind you," Kay said. "I'm Kay." She bent her wrist in a weak hand wave and gave the boy a lips-together smile.

"I haven't seen you here before. Visiting?"

"Yes. I'm staying with Kay and her family. We're from New Jersey."

"I'm not from New Jersey," Kay said. "I moved there a year ago from Florida. Anna's the Jersey girl."

"I used to live in Boston," the boy said. "We moved here four years ago."

Kay folded her arms. "That must've been quite a shock, moving from the big city to a small town like Little Compton."

"Little Compton's a lot different from Boston, that's for sure. We moved here for my dad's job." He jerked his head to the right to shift his wet hair away from his eyes. "Do you girls surf?"

Kay shook her head. "Tried once. Not my sport."

"How about you, Anna?"

She blushed. "Me? No."

"Have you ever tried?"

"No. I'm not a very good swimmer."

"But you can swim a little, right?"

"Yes. A little."

"Then you can learn to surf. Want a quick lesson?"

"I guess…sure. Why not? But the water's pretty cold, and you have a wetsuit on."

"We won't be in the water long," Hank said. "It'll be a quick lesson."

Kay's eyes widened. What was Anna doing? She hated the water; she hated swimming.

"Kay, do you mind if Hank gives me a lesson?"

"That's up to you. Are you sure you want to do this?"

"I won't let anything happen to your friend. We won't be that far out."

Kay backed out of the water, headed down the beach, and yelled back. "Have fun."

CHAPTER EIGHT

"Your knees are blue." Bobbie wrapped a towel around Anna. "Sit in the sun for a few minutes, and then we'll go to the house and get lunch."

Anna dragged her beach chair from beneath the umbrella. "The sun feels good. That water was freezing cold, but surfing was more fun than I thought it would be."

"I saw you stand on the board a few times," Bobbie said.

"Hank told me I wasn't too bad for my first time. Did you see that last run? I stayed on the board almost all the way to the beach."

Kay touched Anna's arm. "What's that?"

"I didn't have my phone, so Hank found a marker in his backpack and wrote his number on my hand. I gave him mine, too."

Kay sat back in the chair and looked over her sunglasses at Anna. "Hmmm. That was quick."

Bobbie tucked her e-reader into her beach bag. "How old is Hank?"

"Fourteen. He'll be fifteen in September. We're the same age. He told me to call him if Kay and I wanted to get together and hang out."

Kay leaned forward in her chair. "Doing what?"

"He said we'd make a fire and cook hot dogs here at the beach some night. Maybe Matt would want to double-date."

Kay glared at Anna. "What? Double-date?"

"Yeah. What's wrong with that?"

"First, I don't know if—"

"Girls, girls. Let's not make any plans yet. Anna, Kay's dad and I are responsible for you, and I don't know if your mom would approve. We don't know much about Hank."

"I went on a date this year. My mom won't mind."

Kay huffed. "If you call meeting a guy at a party at a friend's house with three sets of parents chaperoning a *date*, then, yes, you're right. Remember, we went together—your parents drove us."

"Kay, you said yourself there's nothing to do around here, and Matt said he'd hang with us. If we have the cookout, will you ask him?"

Kay sat silent.

"Did you hear me?"

"Yes, yes. I heard you. If I agree to go to this cookout, I'll ask Matt." Kay slumped into her beach chair. This would be the first time she'd had a date with Matt. All their other meetings had usually been with Anna and were more like fun outings—riding bikes, going to the library in Prospect Harbor, going to pick up Anna at the train station, and even scuba diving. Those seemed natural, with the only expectation to have fun—and, like one of their adventures, also to find gold. She hoped he wouldn't say no.

CHAPTER NINE

Throwing a beach towel across the clothesline, Kay squinted at one of the cottage's windows. "Is that Elena's husband?"

Anna pushed the towel aside. "It must be. Didn't you say only she and her husband lived there?"

"Yes, I did. Don't stare." Kay ducked behind the towel, peeking from the side. "OK. He's gone. Did you see the way he moved back from the window? He disappeared sideways, like he was sliding."

Anna threw another towel over the line. "Maybe he was sitting in his office chair and rolled away."

Kay put a clothespin on the towel and stared at the empty window. "That makes sense."

Bobbie opened the screen door and held out Anna's phone. "Anna, I think it's that boy, Hank; the one you met at the beach."

"Oooh, it's Hank," Kay said, with pursed lips.

Anna ran to Kay's mom. She took the phone, tapped the talk button, and slapped her hand over the device. "Stop it, Kay."

Kay shrugged and walked into the house.

Five minutes later, Anna stepped into the kitchen. "Mrs. Telfair, can Kay and I go with Hank to the beach tomorrow night for a cookout?"

"I still don't know much about this boy," Bobbie said.

"Wait," Kay said. "Who says I'm going? *I* don't want to be a chaperone."

"Ask Matt," Anna said. "You said you'd ask him, remember?"

"Hold it, ladies. I didn't say I approved."

"And I don't know yet if Matt will go," Kay said.

"Please, Mrs. Telfair. Hank said we'd go down there at six and then be home by eight. He told me his dad would drop him off with the wood and the hot dogs and stuff, and he'll call us when everything's set up. Kay and I can ride our bikes down to the beach. We'll be home before dark."

"I'm a little nervous about this." Bobbie pinched her chin. "Kay, do you think Matt would want to go? He's a little older—"

"Not that much older," Kay said.

Anna nodded at Kay's mom. "Matt *is* older, and he and Hank can look after us."

"We don't need *looking after*," Kay said. "I can take care of myself. Besides, Matt might not even want to go."

Bobbie pulled the girls close. She turned to Kay. "You call Matt. If he agrees to go, then you can do the beach cookout."

Reaching across the counter, Kay picked up her phone. Her mouth was dry as cotton. She scrolled through her contacts and tapped the screen.

"Hi, Matt. It's Kay."

CHAPTER TEN

Matt's pickup swayed and bounced hard over the ruts in the un-paved parking area fronting the ocean at South Shore Beach.

"Look, there's Hank," Anna said from the backseat.

Hank motioned to Matt, showing him where to park, and walked up to the truck's passenger window. "Hi, ladies. Ready for some hot dogs and s'mores?" He extended his arm across Kay to shake hands with Matt. "You must be Matt. Anna told me a lot about you and Kay, and how you met in Maine."

"I hope it was—"

"Can we please get out of the truck—now," Kay said. She opened the narrow back door for Anna and whispered to her. "What did you tell Hank?"

"Nothing much. I said you and Matt liked each other."

"Why did you say that?"

"Because it's true."

Hank took the beach chairs from Matt and unfolded them. "Here you go, girls." He chuckled. "Are you going to talk all night, or join the party?"

Kay sat in a chair close to the glowing logs, her body warming and her anger cooling. "The breeze off the ocean's a bit chilly. You've got a good fire going. Feels nice."

Hank dropped another log on the fire and sat next to Kay. "When we met at the beach, you said you moved from Florida to New Jersey, right?"

"Yep. It was a year ago." Kay stared at the burning embers. "I didn't want to move."

"I can understand that. I moved here from Boston in the middle of the school year. Dad lost his job—that's why we moved."

"What does your dad do?"

"He's a civil engineer. He works in construction now. Why did your parents move up North?"

"Kind of the same reason your parents moved here. Dad got a new job." Kay zipped up her sweatshirt. "He said he couldn't pass up the opportunity."

"How did you like moving to New Jersey?"

"Not great at first. I hated to leave my friends."

"Not great?" Anna placed her chair on the upwind side of the fire next to Matt. "Kay, you *hated* it." She grinned. "Until you met me."

"Yeah, right."

"If it weren't for me, you would've been in a lot more trouble."

Hank looked at Anna and then turned to Kay. "What do you mean, 'a lot more trouble'?"

Kay glared at Anna with clenched teeth and took a deep breath. "It was nothing—really."

"That's not what I heard," Matt said.

Kay's eyes bugged, and her face quickly changed to a pleading expression. She shook her head at Matt, her brow drawn tight.

Matt winced. "On second thought, I suppose it wasn't that big of a deal."

"That's right, Matt," Kay said. "It *wasn't a big deal.*"

Anna leaned in closer to the fire. "Kay, you helped the FBI solve a crime, and you almost fell off the Washington Crossing Bridge into the Delaware River. That's not a big deal?"

Hank stopped poking the fire. "Wait, what?"

"Can we drop it." Kay lowered her head, staring out at the rolling surf. "I don't want to talk about this."

"Sorry," Hank said. "Let's cook some hot dogs. Everybody hungry?"

CHAPTER ELEVEN

Bobbie placed her keys and her purse on the counter and turned to Kay. "I met Hank when I dropped Anna off at the beach. He seems like a very responsible boy. I hope I'm doing the right thing letting her go to the beach alone. Are you sure you didn't want to go with them this morning?"

"Two's company; three's a crowd. Besides, I couldn't get up and get going that early. I fell back to sleep after she left." Kay squinted at the kitchen clock. "Wow. I *did* sleep in. It's almost ten."

"You didn't stay long at the beach last night. Did something happen?"

Kay grabbed a mug from the cabinet and shrugged. "We got cold. There was quite a breeze coming off the ocean."

Bobbie held the carafe over Kay's mug. "The fire didn't keep you warm?"

"It was OK. I guess I wasn't in the mood for a cookout."

"Hello?" someone called out, tapping on the screen door.

"Good morning, Elena." Bobbie flipped the door lock. "What's wrong? You've been crying."

"I don't know what to do." The young woman pulled a tissue from her pocket and wiped her eyes. "They tell me I have to move Bramble's paddock. It's too close to where they want to drill the water wells for the new houses."

Bobbie guided Elena to the kitchen "Sit here." She pulled out a stool at the counter. "Want some coffee?"

"I could use some more caffeine, yes. I didn't sleep much last night."

Bobbie poured a cup and slid it in front of Elena. "I can't believe they want you to move the paddock—"

Kay stopped in the middle of a sip of her coffee. "The what?"

"The paddock," her mom said. "It's like a small pasture for horses." She turned to Elena again. "This is a farm. You have a horse. What do they expect?"

Caressing the mug, Elena took a deep breath. "I don't get it either."

"But you were here first," Kay said.

"I know, but there's some ordinance in the town about health and water and…and Zack's not helping matters."

Elena had been coy about Zack during Kay's first meeting with the woman. Burning with curiosity, Kay glanced at her mom and twisted on the stool toward Elena. "What about—"

Bobbie tapped Kay's arm, shaking her head at her ever-inquisitive daughter. She handed Elena the box of tissues.

"I can't deal with all this and Zack, too. Ever since he…" Elena daubed her eyes with the tissue. "I apologize for getting emotional. I don't know what to do. But I'm afraid people won't want to rent the house with the construction going on. To make matters worse, the view from the farm to the river will be the backs of these mini-mansions they're putting up. We need the rent money for expenses. Plus, it's going to cost money to build a new place for Bramble. I'd search for a fulltime job, but Zack…he's…it's not a good time."

Bobbie looked at Kay and then at Elena. "Is there any way you can stop the construction?"

"I don't think so. I've looked into it with one attorney." Elena stared across the room, and then alternated her gaze between Bobbie and Kay. Taking a final a sip of coffee, the woman slid off the stool and walked to the front door. "Sorry to interrupt your morning with my troubles. I guess I had to talk to someone."

Kay stepped out onto the porch. "What are you going to do?"

"There's not much I can do. The landowner has what he wants, and the law seems to be on his side."

"Maybe something from Little Compton's history would make the land valuable," Kay said. "I was reading in this book you left here in the house and—"

"Kay, I'm sure Elena has researched that."

"Yes, and my expensive lawyer, too. There's nothing I can do. Thanks for listening." Elena stepped off the porch and headed toward the cottage.

"There must be something she can do to stop the construction," Kay said.

"Looks like Elena has tried it all," her mom said, turning and walking back into the living room. "I'm sure they wouldn't have started surveying and digging a basement if there was any chance the construction would be stopped."

Kay stood by the door, watching the woman walk to the cottage. She said, in a low voice, "I wish there was something Elena could do. I wish *I* could do something."

CHAPTER TWELVE

S unlight drenched the girls' bedroom. Kay pulled the sheet over her head and then the blanket. "I don't want to be awake."

Anna sat up. "Forget it. It's almost like in Maine last summer. Sun comes up around five thirty." She stretched and gazed out the window. "Somebody's up early over at Elena's. There's a man walking up to the door. He's walking funny, like something's wrong with his legs. He's got a package in his hand, but I can't tell what it is."

Kay tossed the covers back, stepped across to Anna's bed, and stared out the window. "Interesting." She moved closer to the glass. "Kind of a strange-looking character. He needs a haircut and a shave."

Anna peered over Kay's shoulder. "Is he wearing a uniform? Is he maybe in the military?"

Leaning on the sill, Kay squinted. "He's got one of those camouflage jackets with some military patches on it. Maybe he used to be in the military." Kay fell back on the bed and groaned. "It's too early to be thinking. My brain's still asleep."

"Kay, look. Elena's opening the door, and the man's going into the house. Who visits at six o'clock in the morning? Maybe he's delivering illegal drugs, or maybe he's buying them from the Cliffords?"

Kay bolted upright. "What an awful thing to say, Anna. Elena and her husband wouldn't be doing that."

"You said she needed the money from renting the house. She was worried about people not wanting to stay at the farm if the view to the river was blocked."

"That's ridiculous. It's not drugs." Kay shook her head and groaned. "I don't know how you can be so perky this early." She slid her feet into her flip-flops. "I haven't had my coffee yet. There must be some made. I hear my mom and dad."

Kay's dad knocked gently on the door and poked his head in. "I hope we didn't wake you. I have to be at the war college early." He walked over to Kay, sitting on the edge of the bed, and gave his daughter a peck on the cheek. Turning to Anna, he said, "And good morning to you."

"Good morning, Mr.—I mean, Admiral Telfair."

"He's not an admiral, Anna," Kay said. "He's a commander."

"Admiral, commander, whatever—that white uniform is awesome."

"OK, Dad. Go ahead and say it."

Kay's dad picked up his computer bag and winked at his daughter. "I have to go. You all have a nice day."

"Dad, you know what I mean. Say it. You say it every time somebody gives you a compliment on your uniform."

Bobbie entered the room, walked over, grabbed her husband's arm with both hands, and turned to Anna. "Jim says it's the man that makes the uniform, and I agree."

Jim shook his head. "I have to go, ladies." Sporting a wide grin, he pointed at Kay. "And, you—stay out of trouble."

"Not to worry, Dad. You know me. I'm your little angel."

He blew her a kiss. "Love you, kid."

"What about me?" Bobbie put her hands on her hips. The girls joined her, ushering her husband through the kitchen to the back door.

Standing in the doorway, Jim kissed Bobbie and, with a wide grin, waved at Anna. "Love you, too. You're really my favorite."

"Your dad's funny."

"Oh, yes. My dad's a bundle of laughs. Actually, he *is* a lot of fun—most of the time."

Bobbie stepped between the girls. "Any plans today?"

"I'm meeting Hank and his mom at the Landing," Anna said. "That's where the hardcore surfers go. Hank says he's caught some good waves there. Do you want to go, Kay?"

"No thanks. Matt's coming by for lunch."

Anna drew her lips tight. "Oooh, you and Matt are getting chummy."

"Oooh," Kay said. "You and Hank are pretty chummy yourselves."

"Has anyone checked the weather?" Bobbie opened Kay's laptop. "Looks like a chance of rain later today." She made a couple of keystrokes. "Interesting. There's a hurricane in the Caribbean. The forecast says it will hit either Florida or the Carolinas. But the weather people say it's too far away to predict where it will go."

Anna moved next to Kay's mom. "Did you ever go through a hurricane when you lived in Florida?"

"One hurricane did hit us when we lived in Tallahassee," Bobbie said.

"Was it bad?"

"I wouldn't say it was bad, but we had some strong winds and heavy rains. The trees took a beating."

"I don't remember much," Kay said. "I was five or six. I do recall helping Dad pick up the broken tree limbs in the yard after it was over."

Anna took a sip of coffee. "Does Rhode Island ever get hurricanes?"

"Sometimes," Bobbie said. "My grandparents experienced a few. One of the worst happened in 1938. Did a lot of damage, especially along the coast, and it caused a lot of flooding."

"I saw something about that storm in one of Elena's books." Kay went to the shelf. "Here it is." She opened the book and swiped her finger across a page. "The storm hit in September and wiped out most of the buildings at Sakonnet Point. Here's a story from the keeper at the lighthouse: 'At five o'clock all outside doors had been carried away and all windows from the first floor to the third floor were stove in so that we were practically flooded out of our home. At five-thirty I went to the tower to light up. While there, we took what was called a tidal wave. There were seas that went by that completely buried the tower.'"

"That sounds scary," Anna said. "What if one hits Rhode Island while we're here?"

Bobbie stared at the screen. "According to the National Weather Service, this year is supposed to be one of the quietest in decades for hurricanes."

Kay closed the book. "Don't worry, Anna. Most of them hit Florida and other states farther south."

"The chances of us having a hurricane here are pretty small," Bobbie said. "Especially this early in the season, because the water's still cold. But, we have a long way to go. The Atlantic hurricane season lasts till the first of December."

Stopping in front of the bookshelf, Kay opened the volume again and went to the photos of the damage done by the 1938 hurricane. "I hope you're right, Mom."

CHAPTER THIRTEEN

"Thanks for letting me come over, Mrs. Telfair. My nieces and nephews were getting on my nerves." Matt set two large brown bags on the counter. "I brought lunch."

"You didn't have to do that," Bobbie said.

"It was the least I could do to repay Kay for—"

Kay stepped between Matt and her mom and gave Matt the bug-eyed look, along with some quick headshakes. "For...for being nice to Matt when we were in Maine." Kay knew that sounded lame, but she was afraid Matt was going to mention Kay helping him scuba dive for gold. She had never told her mom or dad about the escapade.

Matt stretched his mouth wide and tight—the "oops" expression. "That's right. For all the meals and...and...for letting me hang with your family."

"My goodness, Matt, in Maine you escorted the girls on bike rides, took them boating, and you even brought lobsters and lobster rolls for us a couple of times."

Matt reached into one of the bags. "And guess what I brought. Ta-da. More lobster rolls and lobster mac and cheese."

"I'm starving," Kay said. "Let's eat."

• • •

"That was delicious, Matt. Thanks again. Why don't you and Kay go on the porch, and I'll clean up."

"I can help, Mrs. Telfair."

Kay tugged on Matt's arm. "Come on. *I need help.*"

"Doing what?"

Kay left the porch and returned with her laptop and a stack of books. "I need your help going through some of these books on Little Compton history." She slid a chair under the table, sat, and pulled a book from the stack. "There could be some information in here that might help Elena stop the construction of those houses."

Matt sat on the opposite side. "What exactly are we looking for?"

"Maybe something that shows that the Sakonnets or other tribes lived on that land. If they did, maybe there're some artifacts buried there, and they'd have to declare that it's a historical site."

"You do realize the chances of you finding something are slim," Matt said.

"I know, but I have to try."

Matt picked up the top volume—an American history book for young people—opened the cover, and turned a few pages. "This is interesting." Matt scanned some pages and read: "'More ships came in the three years after the *Mayflower* landed at Plymouth rock. The ships were the *Fortune,* the *Anne,* and the *Little James.*' I don't remember any of this from history classes. It's always been about the *Mayflower.*"

Kay frowned, shaking her head. "Stay on target. I need you to please find stuff on the Sakonnets."

"I will," Matt said, "but here's something else I don't recall studying in American history. Listen to this: 'The Pilgrims were supposed to go to the Virginia Colony, but the ship was blown off course by storms, and it anchored at Cape Cod. When the crew tried to sail south, the weather was bad again, so they sailed back and landed at Plymouth. The ship was made to haul cargo. There were no cabins, no beds, no dining room, and no toilets. Thirty-four children were on the voyage. The passengers also brought dogs, cats, sheep, goats, and chickens. There was no way to wash clothes on the ship. The passengers had to wear the same clothes for more than two months during the trip. The Pilgrims ate salted fish and meat, dried biscuits, peas, fruit, and beans. They drank beer because the fresh water on the ship might make them sick.'"

Kay walked around the table, took the book from Matt's hands, and pushed another in front of him. "Let's get back to our task, please."

"Sorry. I thought that stuff was very interesting."

"It is, and I'd never heard some of that. But we need to focus and find something about the Sakonnets."

Except for a few "hmmms," the teens said nothing to each other for the next fifteen minutes.

Matt pressed his hand across the open book to hold his place. "Even if we know the Sakonnets lived in the area, how will you find any artifacts?"

"Good question. I haven't figured that out yet," Kay said, running her finger across a page. "Everything I've read said the Sakonnets lived in the area in the 1600s and built some of the stone walls." She scratched her head and turned a page. "The Sakonnets had a winter village somewhere near Wilbour Woods. Maybe they had one down by the river in the summer."

Matt flipped back through a few pages. "There might have been some battles here between the tribes, or they fought with the English." His finger swiped back and forth across the page as he read: "'Colonel Benjamin Church fought against the Wampanoag tribe, who were led by Chief Metacomet. Metacomet also had an English name: King Philip.'"

"I read about him, too." Kay scanned a page. "Here it is. Church settled in Little Compton around 1675. That's the year King Phillip's War started. It says here that Church had a good relationship with the Sakonnets, but King Philip wanted the Sakonnets to fight with him against the English." She continued to turn pages.

"Listen to this," Kay said. "'The conflict centered on Indian attacks around the immediate area of Plymouth and quickly spread throughout New England from Connecticut to New Hampshire. The outlying towns in Rhode Island and Massachusetts suffered the worst losses. Philip and his allies killed approximately one-third of the English habitants. Before the war was concluded, thousands of Indian men, women, and children were killed, hung, or sold into slavery.' That's awful."

"War is terrible," Matt said. "My dad and I went to a Memorial Day event in Prospect Harbor last May. One of the speakers told the crowd that there have been almost three million Americans killed and wounded in all the wars since the Revolution. And then he said that there were more people killed in the Civil War than all the other wars combined."

Matt opened another book, and Kay combed through a large volume, flipping back and forth from the index to the inside.

"I'm going to do some searches on the web," Kay said,

More than an hour passed. Matt stacked the books in the middle of the table, leaned in, and placed his hand on top. "There's nothing here that I can find about the Sakonnets living where those houses are going to be built."

"Nothing on the Internet that I could find either." Kay slouched in her chair, closed her computer and the last book she was reading. "Thanks for helping me."

"If you were an archeologist, and they'd let you poke around the land for a few years, you might find something," Matt said.

"Like fossils and things?"

"Exactly. If the Sakonnets had a camp, maybe they left pieces of pottery and tools—anything that would tell you the tribe lived on that land. But I wouldn't know where to start digging. And it's been more than three hundred years since they lived in Little Compton. I doubt these things would be lying on top of the ground. They could be buried deep after all these years. It would take a lot of digging, even if you knew where to dig."

Kay's gaze drifted from the book and down to the construction site. She tapped her chin with her index finger. What if someone else did the digging for you?

CHAPTER FOURTEEN

Kay motioned to Anna from the bedroom doorway. "Come here."

"What is it?"

"How would you like to be an archeologist this evening?"

"I don't think so. I'm a little tired—actually a lot tired. Hank and I surfed till it started raining this afternoon. And did it ever rain." Anna shook her head. "Wait. You said 'archeologist.' You mean digging for stuff? Where did you get that idea?"

"From Matt…kind of."

"He told you to be an archeologist?"

"Not exactly. But he said if we wanted to find any artifacts on the land where the houses are being built, we'd have to dig like archeologists."

"Two questions—why and where?"

"I want to find signs that any of the tribes lived there. If the area is a historical site, maybe the houses can be stopped. We'll search those big dirt piles on the construction site. All we have to do is sift through what they've dug up."

"What do you think your mom and dad will say when you tell them we're going to dig for bones and things?"

"I dropped a hint to mom that she and dad should go out for dinner. Dad's leaving soon to go back home. I told mom they should have some time together. I'll cook for you and me."

Anna lowered her head and arched her eyebrows. "Which means you're not going to tell her."

Kay nodded, made the "zip-it" sign across her lips, and went into the living room.

Bobbie lifted her purse from the back of the chair. "I wasn't sure we'd still be able to go out after that wild rainstorm."

"I believe the rain's passed," Kay's dad said. "The drive here from Newport was awful. We must've had four inches of rain in an hour. I hope this pattern doesn't continue for the rest of your time here."

"The weather guy didn't say anything about rain the next two weeks," Kay said. "But he did say no more rain tonight. Go. Have a good time."

"There's some ground turkey and other stuff in the fridge." Bobbie said. "I feel bad leaving you two here to fend for yourselves."

"Mom, we'll be fine." Kay ushered her parents toward the door. "Please, go and enjoy."

The door clicked shut.

Kay took a deep breath. "Finally."

Anna walked up behind her. "What are you cooking for us tonight?"

Kay rolled her eyes. "Something simple, but after we finish digging."

"It's almost dark. How are we going to be able to see?"

Kay reached into the drawer beneath the counter and took out a large flashlight. "Get your flashlight from the bedroom."

"Kay, this reminds me of—"

"Don't, Anna. I know what you're going to say and—"

"This is crazy."

"It's not. Matt even said it was a good idea."

"Did he say those exact words, 'this is a good idea'?"

"Well, no. Not in those words."

"What'll we dig with?"

"Elena's got some tools next to the shed. I'm sure she won't mind us borrowing them."

Anna sighed. "Here we go again."

CHAPTER FIFTEEN

"The rain is gone," Kay said. "But it's darker than I thought it would be because of all the clouds."

Anna slammed the heel of her sneaker on the ground to knock off the mud. "Will we be able to see anything?"

"I hope so. See that big pile of dirt. I know we can find something there."

The teens walked up to the mound.

Anna stared into the deep hole beside the dirt pile. "Is this a hole for a basement? It looks like a big muddy swimming pool. Yuck."

Using her shovel, Kay dug in the six-foot-high mound of dirt. "Let's see what's in here."

The two girls sifted through the soft earth, neither saying a word.

"We've been at this for twenty minutes, and I don't see anything," Anna said. "Maybe this was a bad idea." She pointed her light at the dirt she'd scattered across the ground. "All I see are some worms."

"Keep digging," Kay said. "It'll be dark soon."

Anna dropped the rake and took a drink from the small bottle of water tucked in her jeans. "It's starting to rain again. I felt a drop. I thought you said it wasn't going to rain anymore?"

"Maybe the weatherman was wrong." Kay moved around and dug on the other side of the dirt mound. "A few drops won't hurt you."

Anna jabbed at the dirt and pulled back clods filled with roots and rocks. She took her flashlight and aimed it at the debris. "What's that?"

Kay shuffled over to the small pile Anna had built. "Looks like a bone. Maybe one of the Sakonnets or Wampanoags was buried here."

"Ewww. A bone. That's awful."

"It's not awful." Holding the bone, Kay held her arm out toward Anna. "This could be what we need."

Anna jumped back. "I don't want to touch that." She screamed, then the sound of splashing water.

"Anna. Anna, where are you?" Kay dropped the bone and shined the light into the swirling water. She jerked the beam of light to point it around the forty-foot square hole. "Where are you?"

"I'm over here." Chest-high in the brownish-gray liquid, Anna coughed, the nasty water dripping off her head.

"I couldn't see you."

"Good reason. I was underwater." Anna raised her arms and shook them. "This is awful. Get me out of here."

"Can't you climb out?"

Anna waded toward the side and reached up. "No. I can't reach the edge. It's slippery anyway. Pull me out, please. There're animals and bugs in here. Hurry!"

"Don't panic. There're no animals and bugs, I promise you." Kay laid the flashlight on the ground, with the light pointing into the hole. She pivoted around, grabbed the rake, and waved it out over the hole, lowering it to Anna. "Grab this, and I'll try to pull you out."

Anna spit and pushed back her wet hair. "Get closer. Can you lower it some more?"

"I'll try." Kay slid each foot across the soggy and slippery ground a few inches at a time, moving closer to the edge of the hole. "I can't get any closer than this."

"Then bend down and get the rake closer to me."

Kay eased down into a squat. "My shoes are sticking in the mud." She lifted her foot and screamed. "Ohhhhh, watch out, Anna!" Kay slid down the side of the hole, feet first, splashing more brown, yucky water over her friend. She stood, rake in one hand and the flashlight beam shooting across the makeshift swimming pool. Only her hair and the upper part of her tank top were left unstained by the water.

The girls stared at each other.

"You were supposed to get me out," Anna said. With a mischievous smirk, she groped in the water and picked up a handful of mud. She held the glob in front of her, staring down at it, and looked sidelong at Kay.

"Don't even think about it." Kay wriggled her feet to step back, but her feet were stuck in the mud. "Anna, don't do it."

Anna lowered her arm, appearing to drop the glob back in the water. Before Kay could react, Anna jerked her arm up and wiped the handful of mud on Kay's top.

Kay stared down at the brown mess, trying to wipe her face with the least muddy hand, and squinted at Anna. Bending down, she shoved her hand into the murky water and pulled up a glob of the mud. She tossed it from hand to hand, some of it oozing between her fingers. "You want to play, huh?"

"Kay, it was a joke. You weren't all covered in this stuff like me."

"A joke?" Kay quickly thrust her arm forward and mashed the slimy ball into Anna's shirt.

"Oh, yeah?" Anna again reached into the mud. "Try this." She waved her hand toward Kay's hair.

Kay reared her head, lost her balance, and fell back into the water up to her neck, supporting herself with the rake to keep from completely submerging.

Anna laughed and pointed. "You look awful."

"Help me up, will you."

Grabbing Kay's hand, Anna leaned back and tugged hard.

Kay grunted, showed that devilish smile, and let go her friend's hand.

Both girls fell back in the muddy soup. Laughing, they grabbed hands, steadied each other, and stood.

Anna pushed her hair back and spit out dirty water. "You're a mess."

"Am not."

"Are, too."

"Am not." Kay eyed the walls of the muddy pit. "We're both a mess, and we'll be in a bigger one if we don't get out of here quick and get back to the house before my parents return."

CHAPTER SIXTEEN

The two mud-caked junior archeologists trudged up the path to the house. Kay used the shovel as a walking stick, and Anna dragged the rake behind her.

"This was one of your worst ideas ever." Anna touched her hair. "I'm never going to get this mud out."

Kay leaned back, shined the light on Anna's head, and picked a tiny twig from her friend's hair. "It adds something. Makes you look... you know...rustic."

"Rustic. More like rusty."

Stopping at the shed near the Cliffords' cottage, Kay said, "Let's leave the tools here, but be quiet."

"Ouch!" Anna let her rake bang against the shed door. "A bug bit me."

A light came on, aimed directly at the girls.

"Hello? Who's there?" Elena stepped onto the back porch of the cottage. "Oh, it's you, Kay. I didn't recognize you at first." She walked up to Anna. "You must be Anna—at least, I think you are somewhere under all that mud."

"Yep. That's her," Kay said. "Mud and all."

"Where've you girls been? You're a little old to be playing in the mud, aren't you?"

"We didn't mean to," Anna said. "We were trying to be archeologists."

Elena rested her elbow in the palm of her left hand and tapped the side of her face. "Archeologists?"

Kay stepped forward, her fingers flicking the caked mud from the front of her top. "We were trying to find things that would prove the Sakonnets lived in the area so we can stop the construction."

"Whatever gave you the idea to do that?"

"It's a long story," Kay said.

"Did you find anything?"

Kay bit her bottom lip, a signal that she had messed up. "I picked up a bone. Or, I thought it was one. But I dropped it."

Elena grinned. "From your appearance, I'd say you literally threw yourselves into the task."

Anna held her arms away from her body. "I started it when I fell in the hole they were digging for the basement of the house."

"I see," Elena said. "And then Kay fell in?"

"She was trying to pull me out."

Elena chuckled. "Looks like that didn't work."

Anna sighed and poked Kay with her finger. "Nope."

"There's a hot water shower on the deck," Elena said. "I'll get some towels, and you both get started washing off all that mud. When you're done, step into the kitchen."

● ● ●

"This is nice," Kay said. "I was getting chilled."

"I warmed the towels in the dryer," Elena said.

Anna pulled her towel up tightly around her. "That warm shower felt good after our swim in that mud pit."

Elena pointed to the stools at the counter. "Have a seat. I made some hot chocolate."

"I love hot chocolate." Anna slid onto the stool and grasped the mug with one hand. She took a sip and struggled to keep the huge towel around her. "What do we do with our clothes?"

"I'll soak them in a tub, and you can get them tomorrow. I hope they weren't good clothes."

Kay was about to take another sip of the chocolate when the kitchen door swung open. With the mug close to her mouth, Kay stopped and held it in midair.

A man in a wheelchair rolled a few inches into the room, stopping under the doorframe. He adjusted the blanket across his lap and stared at the three women, rubbing his beard, first on his left cheek and then on the right.

Elena stepped toward the wheelchair. "This is my husband, Zack."

Anna tugged at the huge bath towel with both hands, bringing it up and under her chin.

Kay set the mug down and raised her hand, palm open. "Hi, Zack. I'm Kay. We're staying next door—me and my parents." She tilted her head at Anna. "And my friend, Anna." Her gaze locked on the wheelchair. She told herself not to stare, but she couldn't stop. Five seconds passed before Kay broke out of her trance-like focus. "Anna and I fell in a hole and..."

Zack backed the chair through the doorway, pivoted with a quick jerk on the wheels, and rolled away.

Elena took a deep breath, her head turned toward the empty doorway. She turned to the girls and forced a smile with barely parted lips. "Want some more hot chocolate?"

"No, no thanks," Kay said. "We should go."

Anna took a final swig from the mug and slid it back. "We'll bring your towels back tomorrow."

Kay moved next to Anna. "Thanks for the shower and hot chocolate...and the towel."

Elena wiped the corner of her eye. "Zack's a little nervous around—"

"We understand...we...I'm..." Kay nodded toward the back door, giving Anna the "let's go" look. She nudged her friend with her elbow. "Thanks again, Elena."

"What? Oh, yeah, sure. You're welcome. Let me get the door. Your hands are full of towel."

"We should have left a light on," Anna said, walking on her tiptoes with Kay toward the house. "Ouch." She stooped and wiped the bottom of her foot. "And I should have brought an extra pair of shoes."

Kay gripped Anna's arm to steady her friend and took a glimpse back at the cottage, the image of Zack Clifford in the wheelchair burned in her mind.

CHAPTER SEVENTEEN

Kay scoured the pan used to make the turkey burgers the night before. Looking out the kitchen window, she called out to Anna in a loud whisper. "Elena's coming over with our clothes."

Anna jumped up from the chair. "Where's your mom?"

"I think she's still in the shower," Kay said, drying her hands.

Anna looked over Kay's shoulder to peek out the window. "She can't find out about this."

"Find out about what?"

Kay jerked her head to the right, looked straight into her mom's face, and flinched. "I didn't know you were standing there."

"Was I not supposed to be here?"

"No, no, Mrs. Telfair. Kay and I were wondering where you were and—"

Elena knocked on the door.

Kay leaned her head back and closed her eyes. This was going to be hard to explain.

"Good morning, Elena," Bobbie said, holding the door wide open for the young woman carrying the clothes basket.

"Good morning, Bobbie. Hi, girls. You look nice and clean today. I hope you don't mind me coming over so early."

Kay's mom stared at the basket and shot a puzzled glance at her daughter. "No, not at all."

Elena placed the basket on the counter. "I rinsed your shoes and put them on the back porch. I soaked the clothes in a tub and ran them through my washer on cold to get out the mud that was left. But the stains might not come out."

Bobbie frowned, reached into the basket, and held up a pair of Kay's capris and a tank top. "I agree. But I have a few questions for my daughter and her friend. Where did you get the stains, and why is Elena doing our laundry?"

Kay winced, her mouth and neck muscles tight, and half-uttered the word "ouch," but it came out more like a stifled hiccup.

Her mom lowered one eyebrow and raised the other. "Are you all right?"

Kay shot a glance at Anna.

Anna turned away, shaking her head.

"Somebody needs to say something." Bobbie moved around to stand in front of the girls.

"I'm sorry, Bobbie. I didn't know the girls hadn't told you."

"Not your fault. It was nice of you to help them." Bobbie placed her hand under Kay's chin and gently lifted it up to get her daughter's attention. "Talk to me."

Kay cut her eyes at Anna.

"Don't look at her. I want to hear from you." Bobbie slid her hand from Kay's chin to her arm. "Again, I'm asking: Why is Elena doing our laundry?"

"Bobbie, maybe I should go."

"No, please stay. Let's have some coffee while I pry some answers from my daughter."

Kay caught Elena's eye. The young woman mouthed the word "sorry."

"It was my fault, Mom. I—"

"Everyone seems to be OK," Bobbie said. "But if it seems like I'm upset...well, I am. My daughter has a knack for getting herself into unusual situations."

Elena pulled a stool toward her and sat. "I can relate to that. My mom went gray in her late thirties because of me, and my dad *lost all* his hair from worrying about me."

Anna shuffled over to Elena. "Really? I can't imagine that you would ever be in trouble."

"Thank you for that vote of confidence, but you'll have to talk with my mom someday. She can tell you stories that would curl your hair."

"Kay's got some of those stories," Anna said.

Kay wrinkled her nose at Anna.

"There's only one story I need to hear," Bobbie said. "The one that evidently was developed last night. Kay, please enlighten me."

• • •

"…and then Elena let us shower and gave us the towels." Tucking her hair behind each ear and then repeating the movement, Kay waited for her mom's response.

"You could have drowned," Bobbie said.

"The water was only chest deep, and I'm a good swimmer."

"That's not the point, Kay," her mom said. "People can drown in a few inches of water." Bobbie shook her head. "You and Anna shouldn't have been down at the construction site, and especially not in the dark. Where did you get the idea to do this?"

"I want to stop those houses from being built somehow. Matt said we'd have to dig to find things that proved the Sakonnets might have lived there. And since those people were digging up the ground for the basement for the new house, I thought maybe there was a chance of finding something."

"Matt said you should do this? That you should go down to the construction site and dig?"

"He didn't say go to that spot, no. He said if we wanted to find any artifacts on the land, we'd have to dig like archeologists."

"And whose idea was it to go to the construction site."

Kay bit her lip. "Mine."

"Then let's not implicate Matt. I'm sure he wouldn't recommend you doing something so reckless."

Anna jumped in. "Yeah, sure, like diving for gold!"

"What was that?"

Kay stepped between Anna and her mom. "She said the water was *cold.*" Kay looked back and gave her friend a glare so intense it could leave a bruise.

Anna swallowed hard. "That's right, Mrs. Telfair. The water was very cold."

"Cold water?" Bobbie shook her head and squinted. "I assumed the water in that pit was cold. That's another thing. You both could've gotten sick."

Elena took the girls' hands and looked back at Bobbie. "They were only trying to help me."

Kay's shoulders drooped, relief spreading across her face. "That's what we were trying to do—help Elena. I can't stand the thought of them destroying the farmland and ruining that beautiful view. You're not going to tell Dad, are you?"

Bobbie nodded toward her daughter. "We'll see."

"I need to go," Elena said. "Zack's waiting for me." She patted Kay on the shoulder. "Thanks for trying, but I don't believe there's any way we can stop the houses from being built. There's nothing more anyone can do."

Standing on the front porch, the three women watched Elena walk toward the cottage. When the young woman was out of hearing range, Kay said to her mom, "We met Elena's husband last night. He was in a wheelchair."

"He was wearing a 'Navy' sweatshirt," Anna said.

"What happened to him?"

"We don't know," Kay said. "Elena didn't say anything except to introduce us, and Zack didn't say anything. He rolled into the kitchen and left in a hurry, right in the middle of when I was talking."

"I guess she'll tell us when she's ready," her mom said. "Let's have some breakfast."

"One more thing, Mom." With a tear running down her right cheek, Kay glanced at Anna and looked at her mom. "Zack doesn't have any legs."

CHAPTER EIGHTEEN

"Thanks for picking me up," Kay said to Matt, sliding into a booth at the restaurant.

Matt slid in across from her. "I'm surprised you didn't want to go to the beach."

"The last few times I was bored sitting and reading with my mom. Anna spent most of the time with Hank and his friends, surfing."

"Everything OK between you and Anna?"

"We're fine. It's us girls being girls. You know." Kay leaned back in the seat. "But, I am worried a little about Elena and her situation at the farm."

"What's she going to do?"

"Nothing. She hired a lawyer, but he said she can't do anything to stop the construction."

"Sounds pretty final to me."

"I know. It's depressing. I want to do something."

Matt unrolled the napkin and laid the knife and fork aside. "What can *you* do? You're certainly not a lawyer; although I have to say, you'd make a good one. You don't give up...on anything."

"Thanks...I guess."

"I mean that as a compliment. I've never met anyone so determined to do something once her mind is made up."

"My dad calls it being headstrong. He says it can be a good character trait if I know when to use it."

Matt nodded. "Was he referring to the Washington Crossing adventure?"

"That and lots of other situations."

"Yeah, but you helped solve a crime at the park visitors center. And in Prospect Harbor you helped me find the gold that paid for my new truck, part of my college, and my mom's medical bills. I'd say being headstrong worked out."

"True, but I push it too far sometimes."

The two teens scanned the menus and told the server their orders.

"What could we do to help Elena stop the houses from being built?" Kay peeled the paper off her straw. "Windcrest Farm is so beautiful. And what a fantastic view of the Sakonnet River, flowing out to the ocean."

"I assume the lawyers looked at the deeds." Matt drummed his fingers on the table. "But there was a situation somewhere in New England where a company wanted to put up a building, and they discovered that there had been a Native American village or something on the construction site. Whatever it was, the construction had to stop."

"There's got to be a way to find out if the Sakonnets ever lived on that land." Kay wasn't yet ready to tell Matt about the incident at the construction site.

A gray-haired man, wearing large black-framed glasses sitting in the booth behind them, turned and placed his arm on the seat back. "Excuse me. I couldn't help but hear your conversation. Let me introduce myself. I'm Hanscomb Bolles. I've done some research on the indigenous peoples in New England."

Kay slid farther into the booth, twisted her body to the right, and faced the man. "Indigenous?"

Bolles gave a polite smile. "The original inhabitants. The people who were here when the English came over from Europe."

Kay cut her eyes at Matt and then turned to Bolles. "Are there any places where the ingid—"

"Indigenous," Bolles said.

"Right. Do you know of any places around here where these people lived?"

Bolles pursed his lips and tilted his head toward Kay. "Do you have a specific location in mind?"

"Windcrest Farm," Matt said.

"Ah, the Cliffords' place. Beautiful location."

"Not for long," Kay said. "Somebody's building a bunch of big houses close to the river."

"I don't know of any archeological sites near the farm. I'm sure if there were, no construction would be allowed."

"Maybe nobody ever did a search," Kay said.

Bolles smiled and adjusted his glasses on his nose. "Maybe."

Matt leaned forward, his forearms on the table. "If we wanted to do some research ourselves, where would we go?"

"I have several papers that I wrote on the indigenous peoples when I was working on my doctorate degree at the University of Rhode Island. I'll be happy to answer any questions you may have." He reached into his pocket. "Here's my card, the one I used when I was teaching."

"Excuse me, folks," the server said. "Who gets the grilled cheese?"

Matt raised his hand.

"Then this is for you, young lady. Enjoy."

Kay spun her plate around to get at the french fries and turned back to the man. "What do you do now?"

"I dabble in a few things—make a few investments here and there. Something to keep me busy." Bolles rose from his booth and faced the teens. "Nice talking with you."

Taking a quick glance back as the man stepped out the door, Matt leaned in. "That was an interesting conversation."

"Very." Kay pulled her napkin from her lap, blotted her mouth, and dropped the cloth on the table. She squinted, eyeing Bolles, who strolled past the window in front of the restaurant. "There's something else I need to tell you. It's about me and Anna and the construction site."

"Now what did you do?"

Kay explained the muddy adventure and how she and Anna met Zack. "I'd never known anyone who lost an arm or leg. It made me sad."

"That is tragic," Matt said. "I'll bet he lost them on some dangerous mission in Iraq or Afghanistan."

"Maybe." Elena didn't seem to want to talk about it, and we didn't ask."

"And speaking of dangerous," Matt said. "That adventure at the construction site was a bit dangerous, don't you think?"

"Yes, and stupid. But I thought we would find some artifacts, like when we found the gold."

"Going after the gold was different. We had some clues—the letter and other information." "How do we get some clues here?"

Matt pulled the napkin from his lap and laid it on the table. "Maybe one of the property owners from the past would know some of the history of the area. Some of these farms have stayed in one family for generations."

"That's *it*," Kay said.

"What's *it*?"

"Want to do some detective work?"

CHAPTER NINETEEN

"How can I help you?" The woman drew her hands back from the computer keyboard.

Kay leaned on the counter. "May we please see the deed for the land that's next to Windcrest Farm?"

The woman peered at them from over her glasses. "The Calder parcel?"

"I guess that's the one, yes," Kay said. "It's where they're building those big houses."

"There's been a lot of interest in that land the past few years." The woman walked toward a wall of file cabinets. "Do you need a copy of the deed?"

"No. No, we...I mean...I don't need a copy. I just wanted to look at it."

The woman walked to the bank of file cabinets and pulled open a drawer. "Are you two buying one of the houses?"

Kay's mouth dropped. "Us? Me?" She felt the heat from her face. "We're not...I'm fourteen—soon to be fifteen. I'm tall, and that makes—"

"We're friends of the Cliffords," Matt said. "We wanted to find out who owned the land next to them before it was last sold."

The woman closed the file drawer. "I can tell you that without pulling up the deed. It was Samuel Calder. His family's been in Little Compton a long time." She tapped the side of her face. "Come to think of it, somebody named Calder passed away last year. I think it was him. I believe he's buried in the cemetery across the street."

"Thanks." Kay smiled and led Matt out of the office and down the stairs. "That wasn't much help. Let's cut through the cemetery to your truck and see who this Calder person is who's buried there."

Kay led the way through the low, iron gate and into the cemetery. "These headstones are hundreds of years old. Some of them you can hardly read. The date on that one is 1642."

"There's a tall one," Matt said.

Kay walked around the eight-foot-high granite monument and read the inscription: "'Elizabeth Pabodie, daughter of the Plymouth Pilgrims, John Alden and Priscilla Mullin, the first white woman born in New England.'"

Peering from around the other side, Matt also read: "'Here lyeth the body of Elizabeth, the wife of William Pabodie, who died May thirty-first, 1717 and in the ninety-fourth year of her age.'"

"I vaguely remember this from American history class," Kay said.

Matt walked away.

Kay knelt and read more of the monument's inscriptions. "Listen to this, Matt." Kay craned her neck around the side of the monument. "Matt?"

"Over here. Look at this."

Kay moved around in front of the headstone, a newer slab of granite that was unlike most of the other weathered and stained memorials in the cemetery. "'Adeline Calder, beloved wife.' She died two years ago." Her eyes scanned to the right. "There's Samuel Calder's name, but there's no date when he died."

"Maybe they haven't gotten around to adding the date," Matt said. "The woman at the town clerk's office said she thought he died last year."

"Actually, she said *somebody* named Calder died last year. Maybe it was his wife who passed away." Kay tapped her chin with her index finger. "Assuming she's right, why would it take this long to add the date when *Mr.* Calder died?" She mumbled to herself. "Doesn't make sense."

CHAPTER TWENTY

Anna squeezed in the space on the loveseat next to her friend. "I forgot to ask last night, how was lunch with Matt?"

"OK. We met a guy in the restaurant who said he'd studied the Sakonnets, and then we walked through the cemetery."

"Wow. Sounds like an exciting date."

"It wasn't a date."

"If you say so."

Kay's mom and dad agreed that she couldn't date till she was fifteen, and only after they had met the boy's parents. But her mom had met Matt's parents. "OK, technically it was a date," Kay said, hammering her laptop with rapid keystrokes.

"What *are* you doing? I thought we were going to the beach. Your mom's got the beach bag packed. Hank's going to meet us. He's probably there now. Let's go."

"I'm coming, but first I need to do a search."

"For what?"

"I want to find out who owned the property where those houses are being built."

"Kay, you're exasperating."

"I know." Kay put on her widest Cheshire Cat grin. "That's what makes me so lovable."

"I'm going to put my towel and stuff in my backpack. Hank said he would bring me a wetsuit—his mom's. I was freezing the last time we went surfing."

Kay grunted.

Anna put her hands on her hips. "Are you listening to anything I say?"

"What? Sure." Kay said, staring at the computer screen.

"I'm going to run away with Hank to Madagascar."

Fingers hovering above the keyboard, Kay focused on the content popping up on the screen. "Sounds nice. Enjoy."

Anna walked away. "You're impossible. I'm going to put my suit on."

Shaking her head, Kay chuckled and said in a low voice, "Madagascar? Where did she come up with that?"

Her brain in overdrive, Kay's focus was on finding Samuel Calder— if he was alive. Mumbling to herself, her eyes danced back and forth across the screen. "There's nothing on Samuel Calder, only an S. Calder and an odd-sounding address."

Kay looked up from the computer. "Mom, someone's at the door."

No answer.

Making a few more keystrokes, Kay pulled her hands off the keyboard and walked to the door.

"I have a package for B. Telfair," the postman said. "I know this is a rental house. May I see some identification, please?"

"Sure." Kay went to her mom's purse on the nearby table and returned with her mom's driver's license. "Excuse me. You must know the streets here in Little Compton. Can you tell me how to find this place? I can't find it on any map." Kay rattled off the strange address.

"It's a private road off another private road. It's next to Wilbour Woods." The man took out a piece of paper and drew a map.

"This is great. Thank you." Kay went back to her computer. "Now, we're getting somewhere."

CHAPTER TWENTY-ONE

"**B**ye, Dad." Kay reached up to give him her typical light-fingered, pat-on-the-back hug.

"That's all I get? I won't see you for two weeks. Give me a real hug."

Kay grinned and wrapped her arms around her dad. "I wish you could stay till we all leave."

"Me, too. But I did my time with the navy this summer, and now work beckons. And don't forget—I have a trip to Japan coming up. I leave Monday. Besides, I want to save some of my vacation time for our trip in August." Jim picked up his bag and computer case. "OK, I'm off. By the way, I saw on the weather last night that the hurricane has a fifty percent chance of going toward Bermuda and turning into a tropical storm. But you could get some wind and rain if it gets a little closer. I hope it doesn't spoil your last few weeks here."

"We can always download some e-books," Bobbie said.

Kay held up her smartphone. "And there's always the Internet."

Anna pointed at the flat screen. "And TV."

Kay's dad checked the computer case latch and then looked at Anna. "What if you lose power?"

"That's *our* problem." Bobbie kissed her husband and nudged him toward the door. "We'll be fine. Get moving, dear. I don't want you to leave, but if you want to beat the afternoon rush hour on I-95 through Connecticut, you'd better get going."

Jim went over to his daughter, whispered something in her ear, and dashed for the door. "Bye, all."

"Bye, Dad," Kay said, plopping on the sofa with her laptop and throwing him an arm wave.

Anna sat by her friend on the sofa. "What was that about?"

"Just some advice."

"Personal, huh?"

"No. He said not to feel bad if I get 'stonewalled' while trying to help Elena."

"What's that?"

"Stonewalled?" Kay tapped on the keyboard. "It means 'getting stopped or having somebody or something keep you from doing what you want to do.'"

"That's funny. I mean not hilarious funny, but weird funny—you know, with all the stone walls around here."

Bobbie walked over to the girls. "The word is ironic. Jim finds irony and humor in everything."

"Speaking of finding things," Kay said in a low voice. "I need to text Matt about something." She typed, "Hi, Matt. Do you want to go find out if Mr. Calder's still alive?"

CHAPTER TWENTY-TWO

The red pickup bounced in and out of the ruts in the dirt road, which was more like a cow path through a pasture.

"Are you sure this is the way to Calder's house?" Matt jerked the wheel to avoid a deep hole.

Kay gripped the door's armrest. "The postman gave me the directions. He acted like he was very sure on how to get here."

Kay moved closer to the windshield and pointed. "Over there's a 'no trespassing' sign."

Matt stopped the truck. "Do you want to keep going?"

"Yes. We've come this far."

"Here we go. Hang on."

Kay's body lurched from side to side, the seatbelt cutting into her neck. "I feel like I'm on a ship in a storm."

Five minutes later, a hard left turn put the truck and its occupants in front of a house covered in weathered, cedar shingles. Some of the shingles were missing near the house's peak, and a broken downspout hung lifeless from the rain gutter. The garage beside the house was near collapsing. A narrow dirt path led up to the house, where half of the first step was missing from the stairs that led to a small porch.

"I don't believe anybody lives here," Kay said. "Maybe Calder *has* passed away."

Matt pointed across Kay and out the passenger window. "Somebody in that family lived here at one time. That old wooden sign says 'Calder.'"

Kay reached for the door handle, but hesitated. "Should we go knock on the door?"

"It's your decision, Detective Telfair." Matt grinned. "I'm only a lowly detective's assistant."

"Very funny.

"It's true. You're a natural detective."

"OK. OK. You and Anna." Kay shook her head. "You both are—"

"What do you want?" A man with a scraggly, salt-and-pepper beard stood at the driver's door. He carried an old and splintered baseball bat, raising it and slapping it in the palm of his hand.

Matt pushed himself back in the seat, looking left at the man.

Wearing a ball cap and dressed in faded blue overalls, the man dragged his fingers through his untrimmed beard.

Kay's hands shook, her mouth bone dry. "I…we…we wanted to talk with Mr. Samuel Calder."

"That's me. Talk about what?"

"The land you sold near Windcrest Farm."

"What about that land?"

Kay's voice cracked. "I have a few questions about the history and the Sakonnet tribe."

The man eyed the teens, backed away, and scanned Matt's truck front to rear.

Kay squirmed in her seat, her eyes wide, and looked at Matt.

Calder dropped the bat by his side and motioned toward the house. "Come inside if you want. Anybody who took the time to come way out here in these woods to see me is worth talking to." Calder held up the bat. "Sorry about this—it's my protection," he said, in a gravelly voice. "I get some unwanted visitors out here sometimes." He lowered the bat and leaned on it like a walking cane, making his way with halting steps up the stairs to the porch and into the house.

Standing three feet past the front door, Kay scanned the room, her mouth as wide as the opening of a large mayonnaise jar. Framed photos of men in military uniforms and military equipment and boats covered one wall of the room. Neat rows of photos of weddings and family events lined a narrow table. She and Matt sat on a battered sofa with mismatched pillows.

Calder rested the bat against the wall and sat in an equally well-worn recliner. "Young lady, you said you had some questions about that piece of land?"

"You know they're building big houses on it."

"I'm aware."

"Don't you think it's terrible that those homes will spoil the view down to the river? And they'll probably tear down the stone walls, too."

The man took in a deep breath and looked away. "It's not my concern."

"My family's renting a house at Windcrest Farm, and the owner says she won't have as many renters in the future if the view of the river is blocked. And that means she loses money."

Calder rubbed his finger across his upper lip, as if scratching an itch. "I agree. It's a shame that land isn't being farmed. And, you're right, the view will be spoiled. I'm sorry for the owner of the farm. But it's not my land anymore. I can't do anything about it."

Kay glanced at Matt. "We understand that. But if some Indian artifacts are buried on the land, maybe the construction can be stopped."

Matt jumped in. "Maybe the land was used for a village or a camp."

Calder reached over and lifted the framed photo of a young man in a navy uniform and a young woman in a wedding dress. "I sometimes regret selling that land. I inherited it from my parents. They had farmed it since the 1940s, and their parents and grandparents a hundred years before that." He set the frame back on the table. "My wife and I had planned on selling this place and building a small cottage over there. She did love that view." He turned to Kay. "But what's done is done."

Calder sat back in his chair and reached down and pulled up his right pant leg. "These things are great, but they aren't perfect." He twisted and adjusted his prosthetic leg and pushed the pant leg down.

Kay couldn't stop staring. If her mom were here, she would say: "It's not polite to stare." But her Mom wasn't here, and this was the first time Kay had ever seen an artificial limb up close. She'd seen the ads on TV for military veterans who were wounded, but she'd never known anyone who'd lost a limb until she saw Zack after the disastrous archeology dig.

Raising his left pant leg, Calder revealed another artificial leg. After making a few adjustments, he raised his head and chuckled. "I wanted a matched pair. One would be a bit odd, don't you think?"

Kay swallowed hard. "A pair? I guess…I don't—"

"I'm kidding. Sorry if I made you uncomfortable. After I lost my legs it took me a year to accept the fact that I would have to wear these things if I was going to try and lead a normal life. Took a while, but now I don't care if people stare at the way I walk. It's natural for them to do that. I don't blame them."

Kay locked her gaze on a photo on the wall of five young men in their twenties, standing on the deck of a boat. "How did it happen— losing your legs?"

"I was in Vietnam in 1969 in the navy. A rocket-propelled grenade hit my boat during a river patrol, and I was standing next to where the round hit." He nodded and stared at the same photo that had caught Kay's attention. "But enough about my legs." He laughed and slapped both. "You asked the history of that land."

Kay put her hands together beneath her chin. "Do you know anything that could help us?"

"I know one of my great-grandparents had heard stories of Sakonnets and Wampanoags living around that area. They fished in the river and planted corn and such. These are word-of-mouth stories, mind you. I'll bet you can find more information at the Little Compton Historical Society." Calder drew his mouth up and squinted. "Funny you should ask about this property, though. Somebody came to see me last year, asking about it."

Matt looked at Calder. "Who was that?"

"Let me see. What was his name?" Calder opened a drawer on the end table and retrieved a tattered notepad. "Here it is." He put on his glasses, struggling with one hand. "His name was Bolles."

"We met him a few days ago," Matt said.

Kay made eye contact with Matt for a split second and sat forward in her chair. "What did he ask you?"

"Same things you asked me about."

"Did he say why he wanted the information?"

"Said he was doing research on Native Americans in Little Compton. He was a professor. Yep, I remember—a retired history professor."

"Interesting." Kay stood and extended her hand. "Thanks for your time, Mr. Calder."

Matt shook hands with Calder and followed Kay out the door.

"That's a nice pickup," Calder said, walking out behind them. He pointed to the side of the house. "I need to get mine running. Needs a part or two."

"The older trucks do need a lot of maintenance." Matt opened the door, hopped in the driver's seat, and stuck his head out the window. "I used to work a lot on my *old* truck to keep it running."

Calder grinned. "If you ever want to work on another old pickup, you know where I live."

"Thanks for bringing me out here," Kay said, climbing into the truck. "This Bolles guy, don't you think—"

"Do I think it's a coincidence that Bolles was here last year?" Matt slid the key into the switch and turned to his friend. "Chances are it's a coincidence."

"I guess you're right. Professor Bolles wasn't too encouraging. He'd done some research. But still…" Kay put her left hand to her face and tapped her lip with her little finger.

Waving at Calder, Matt started the engine and backed out onto the dirt road. "But what?"

"I don't know." Kay stared out the passenger window. "It's probably nothing."

CHAPTER TWENTY-THREE

"**I** thought you were going to the admissions office at URI today," Kay said, opening the screen door for Matt.

"I decided not to go and came to see if you were leaving before the storm hits."

"We aren't planning to go anywhere," Kay said. "It could be only a tropical storm by the time it gets close to New England, and it might not be that strong."

"That's true, but we still could get some nasty weather," Matt said. "The winds are picking up. I checked the weather radar before I left my aunt's, and it shows a band of rain showers headed this way."

Elena cracked the door. "I saw Matt's truck in the drive. Are you leaving? It looks as if the storm could hit Little Compton."

"No. We're staying," Bobbie said. "But since you asked, should we? Are you leaving?"

"No, no. Zack doesn't want to leave. But we could lose power. The only generator we have is wired into this house."

"If the electricity goes out, you and Zack can come stay with us," Bobbie said.

"Thanks, but let's hope the storm won't be that bad."

Matt's gaze went back and forth between Bobbie and Elena. "Since you're all staying, I can help with whatever needs to be done to get ready."

"We have shutters that can be closed on some of the windows on this house and in the cottage," Elena said. "And we should move any loose items indoors."

Bobbie looked at Matt. "What about your aunt's house?"

"The house is buttoned up like a winter coat. My uncle and I have been prepping for a week, just in case."

Anna stepped through the bedroom doorway and into the living room. "What's this I hear about a hurricane and closing shutters?"

Kay pursed her lips and made a swooshing sound. "It's a hurricane, Anna. A terrible hurricane. Lots of wind and rain. It'll be awful."

The color drained from Anna's face. Her mouth fell open.

Bobbie moved over and put her arm around Anna. "Kay, that was mean."

Kay caught Matt's eye. Her friend from Maine shook his head.

Kay winced. "Sorry, Anna. I was only trying to be funny."

Bobbie used her compassionate, motherly tone. "Anna, we were talking about what we should do to prepare in case the storm hits us."

"Are we going to have a hurricane?"

"We're not sure." Kay moved to the small desk and opened her laptop.

"Is anyone hungry?" Anna rubbed her tummy. "I haven't had any breakfast."

"Elena, would you like to stay and have some blueberry pancakes? Do you want some, Matt?"

A buzzing noise erupted from Elena's jeans pocket. She pulled out her phone and poked the screen. "I need to run, but thanks for the invitation."

Matt raised his hand. "I'm for pancakes."

Bobbie opened the fridge door. "Kay, would you grab the pancake mix from the cupboard, please?"

Pounding on the keyboard, Kay never looked up.

"Kay, did you hear me?"

"You need to see this," Kay said.

Anna, Matt, and Bobbie stood behind Kay.

"That's quite a change from last night," Bobbie said.

Matt nodded. "That's a big change from a few hours ago."

Kay focused on the screen. "Should we call Dad?"

Bobbie stepped back from the desk. "He's already on his way to Tokyo, or he might even be there by now. Let's have some breakfast and then talk about what we should do."

CHAPTER TWENTY-FOUR

"Thanks for the pancakes, Mrs. Telfair," Anna said, putting her breakfast dishes in the sink.

"They were delicious," Matt said.

Kay took her coffee mug and walked to the computer. "Let's check the weather report again." She sat and swiped the laptop's touch screen. "They're predicting a good chance the storm will stay a hurricane and will come on land somewhere on Long Island or Connecticut. But it could hit land anywhere from New York to Massachusetts. "

"Rhode Island is in the middle," Anna said. "It's like we're the center of the target for the hurricane—a bull's-eye."

"Even if it doesn't hit us directly, we *will* get some wind and rain," Matt said.

Kay's mom lifted the top of the coffee maker and poured in water. "My target is more coffee. I need a second cup. Then we can focus on what we need to do to get ready in case the storm hits us hard." She turned to Matt. "Not that I want you to leave, but shouldn't you get to your aunt's house before the weather gets nasty?"

"I'd like to stay here as long as I can and help you, if that's OK."

"Of course. You could even stay the night, if you like." Bobbie grinned and pointed at Kay and Anna. "These are the only bratty kids you'd have to contend with."

"Mom, that's not nice."

"I'd love to stay over." Matt winked at the girls. "These two aren't quite as demanding as my four nieces and nephews. I'll call my aunt and let her know."

Anna's phone jingled. She walked away talking and came back to the living room. "It's Hank. He wants to go surfing. He says the best waves happen ahead of the storm. "Can I go, Mrs. Telfair?"

Bobbie moved around in front of Anna. "Please tell Hank that it's best that you don't go today. It's too dangerous."

"The waves can be unpredictable," Matt said. "My dad and I found out the hard way. We were lobster fishing a few hours ahead of a storm and had a tough time getting back to Prospect Harbor. We hit some huge waves that broke over the boat."

"I guess you're right. I'm not that experienced."

"That's for sure," Kay said. "I'd hate to have to come rescue you or call out the Coast Guard."

Anna stuck her tongue out at Kay. "I wouldn't want to bother you."

Bobbie clapped her hands. "Everyone, let's focus on what we need to do to get ready for the storm."

"Since you're an expert at getting ready for hurricanes, Matt, how about you closing the shutters," Kay said. "Anna and I will pick up the loose stuff outside."

Bobbie let her gaze drift to the kitchen window. "What about Elena's horse?"

"When we finish with stuff around the house we can go see if she needs help," Kay said.

• • •

Matt struggled to close the barn door.

Elena stepped up beside him and gave an extra push to move the door in place. "I've been meaning to fix these hinges and the latch." She turned to the three teens. "Thanks for helping get Bramble in the barn and closing the shutters. Zack was worried about me doing that by myself."

Anna moved close to Elena. "Will you and Zack be OK in the cottage?"

"I hope so. Let's pray the storm calms down before it reaches New England."

Kay covered the left side of her face with her hand to block the wind-driven rain. "Call us if you need us."

The three teens walked, heads down, back to the house.

Walking behind Matt and Anna, Kay stopped. With her back to the wind, she pulled her phone from her pocket, swiped the screen, and shouted over the wind. "More bad news."

CHAPTER TWENTY-FIVE

Minutes after a dead calm outside, raindrops the size of grapes pelted the side of the house.

"That's scary." Kay said. "Sounds like firecrackers going off. I wish we had shutters on *every* window."

Matt peered out the kitchen window, one of the two not covered by a shutter. "The rain won't break the glass, but hail or a flying object could do some damage."

Anna's eyes widened. "Hail? In a hurricane?"

Kay leaned back on the arm of the sofa. "And sometimes tornadoes. That's what that lady said on the weather station."

"Let's calm down." Bobbie sat in front of the computer. "The storm is still a few hours away."

"Shouldn't we have gone home?"

"It's too late now, Anna," Matt said. "The Rhode Island State Police said that people shouldn't be travelling except for emergencies."

"So we're stuck here? What if the storm hits Little Compton?"

"I think we're as prepared as we can be," Bobbie said. She rubbed her chin with her thumb and index finger and lifted her head to peer over the computer screen. "The next hurricane tracking report is coming soon."

Five minutes passed.

Bobbie typed on the keyboard and leaned in toward the screen. Her blank expression changed to the "worried mom" look.

Kay put her head close to the screen. "What's wrong?"

"It's a category one hurricane, and it's going to make landfall near Westerly."

"That means the bad side of the storm will pass over Little Compton," Matt said.

"What should we do?" Anna swallowed hard. "The wind is pretty strong *now.*"

"We do what my dad always says when a storm is coming," Kay said. "Batten down the hatches."

Anna put her hands on her hips. "And that means?"

Matt smiled. "It means tie down the loose stuff outside—which we've done—and hang on for a rough night."

Kay jerked her head left and right. "Was that the lights flickering?"

A flash of lightning lit up the room, then the lights went out.

Anna covered her mouth and let out a muffled scream through her clenched fists.

"I'll start the generator," Matt said. He shined a light around the room, which was dark even in early afternoon with the closed shutters and the heavy cloud cover outside.

"Take this." Kay shoved a small flashlight into Anna's hand. "Don't worry."

Ten minutes later, Matt stood in the kitchen, shaking the water droplets from his jacket. "The generator's only wired into the kitchen and maybe one or two other outlets. It'll run a few lights and, I'm hoping, the fridge."

Bobbie opened the refrigerator door. "The light's on, and we have the gas stove. We won't starve. And we have a few candles."

Anna reached into the bedroom and flipped the wall switch. "No lights in the bedroom. We'll have to sleep in the dark."

Bobbie walked over to Anna and pulled her close. "Did you forget that you normally sleep in the dark?"

"Oh, yeah. But sometimes I have a nightlight, and I've never been in a hurricane. I'll admit it. I'm scared." Anna jumped. "What's that banging noise?"

Kay's mom steadied the young girl. "It's the door. Someone's at the door."

"It's Elena." Kay unlocked the door and held on tight to keep the wind from blowing it wide open.

Elena stepped inside and flipped the hood of her rain jacket off her head. "Zack's very anxious. The wind noise. The lightning. I thought we'd be OK, even without electricity, but I guess not. He saw the lights over here. I don't know what else to do."

"Why don't you both come over here," Bobbie said.

"I guess that'll be OK. I need to tell you that Zack is sometimes not that comfortable being around people he doesn't know."

Bobbie smiled at Elena. "We have room. Please come stay with us."

"Thanks. I might need help. Let me think." Elena pressed on her forehead with the tips of her fingers. "We'll have to come in through the back door with the wheelchair. We have some ramps in the shed; we haven't had a chance to make this place wheelchair-accessible yet."

With her head moving no more than an inch or two in any direction, Kay cut her eyes from her mom, to Matt, and then to Anna. This was the first time Elena had mentioned Zack's use of a wheelchair.

"Listen," Bobbie said. "There's a break in the rain."

Kay grabbed her windbreaker from the coat rack. "Matt and I'll go with Elena."

"Anna and I will get the ramp from the shed," Bobbie said.

• • •

Elena held the door open. Matt and Kay pulled on the chair handles, wrestling the chair through the opening.

The wheels bumped over the sill and jostled Zack.

Elena tugged at the young man's sweatshirt hood, trying to remove the hood.

His head down, Zack resisted and pulled the hood farther over his head, almost covering his eyes. He grabbed the chair's handrims, spun around, and pushed off toward the living room.

"He doesn't say much," Anna said in a soft whisper. "I hope we don't make him uncomfortable."

Kay stared at the back of the chair. Uncomfortable for Zack? This could be uncomfortable for everyone.

CHAPTER TWENTY-SIX

The weather alert radio beeped and crackled: "Winds approaching seventy-five miles per hour are expected to hit southern New England over the next twelve hours. Bands of rain and tornadoes are possible as the storm passes. Residents should—"

Kay lowered the volume and moved from the desk to the sofa, sitting next to her mom with Anna on the other side.

Bang! The walls of the house shook.

Zack rotated his chair in a circle.

Elena jumped up and knelt beside the chair, touching Zack's arm. She scanned the teens' faces. "Very loud noises upset him. I'll bet it's that red oak. I should have had it trimmed. The tree's grown too close to the house, and it—"

A scraping noise echoed through the living room.

"What was that?" Kay cupped her hands to her ears. "It sounds like a giant hand's trying to tear open the side of the house."

Matt placed his head close to the kitchen window. "It's that tree limb. The wind's blowing it against the house. It could bang against the house all night. We should cut it loose before the wind gets any stronger."

"Let me see." Kay tugged at Matt's arm and looked out the window. "How would you cut it? It could be dangerous."

Matt grabbed another look. "Elena, do you have a saw?"

"Yes, in the generator shed. But you don't have to do this. I agree with Kay; it's too dangerous."

"I can do it."

Bobbie craned her neck by the window to get a glimpse of the flailing limb, thumping hard like a drumbeat. "Are you sure you can do this?"

"Yes," Matt said. "There's a piece of the limb holding it to the tree. A couple of swipes with the saw and it'll fall."

Elena walked to the window, pressing her face close to get a better view. "If you think you can do it. Please be careful."

"If it's OK with you, Mom, I'm going with Matt to help him."

Bobbie took a deep breath. "What do you think, Matt?"

"It wouldn't be a bad thing to have someone watching out for me. I'll be focused on sawing."

"You'd better hurry," Elena said. "It'll be dark sooner this evening with the clouds and all the rain."

A smaller limb broke from the huge tree and slapped the glass. Kay jumped back, her heart pounding. "Let's go, *now*."

CHAPTER TWENTY-SEVEN

Matt stepped out of the shed with the saw in one hand and the ladder in the other. He pulled Kay close. "Close the latch so the door doesn't blow open. We don't want the generator to get wet."

"What?"

"I said…" Matt pointed at the free-swinging door and made a twisting motion with his hand.

Kay locked the door and yanked on the handle. She picked up one end of the ladder and walked with Matt to the oak tree.

Matt stared up at the limb for ten seconds and turned back to Kay, putting his mouth close to her ear. "Don't let go the ladder. The wind's really bad."

Kay covered her face to block the stinging rain, nodded, and gave him the OK sign, the same one she had used underwater while diving for gold in Maine. She tugged on his rain jacket and placed her head beside his ear. "Be careful!"

Climbing the ladder, Matt planted each foot on the slippery rungs, testing the foothold before moving on. He looked down at Kay and thrust the saw up toward the limb.

Dodging the sawdust blown by the wind, Kay tilted her head back to check Matt's progress. He stopped sawing and looked down. Shaking his head, he pointed at his arm and flexed, mouthing the word "tired."

Kay nodded and wiped her face with both hands.

In the few seconds Kay had let go her grip on the ladder, a gust of wind hit Matt. His body acted like a sail on a ship's mast, and he and the ladder drifted away from the tree. Holding on to the saw with one hand and the ladder with the other, Matt was helpless to stop the motion of his perch.

Grabbing the rails of the wobbling roost, Kay leaned hard against it, but could only stop the ladder's movement. She couldn't push it back toward the tree. The teen looked up and saw the panic in Matt's eyes. She moved behind the ladder, grabbed a rung up high, and used her whole body weight to pull her friend back toward the oak. Matt let go the ladder, extended his arm, and grabbed one of the tree limbs.

Keeping her grip on the ladder, Kay closed her eyes and shook her head to clear the raindrops from her face. A warm, moist burst of air hit the back of her neck. She screamed.

CHAPTER TWENTY-EIGHT

Kay spun around. "Bramble. You're loose!"

Making the final cuts on the limb, Matt threw the saw away from the tree and scurried down the ladder.

Grabbing Matt by the sleeve, Kay ran her hand over the horse's left leg and shouted over the wind. "We have to get him back in the barn. He's been cut."

"I'm not a horse person," Matt said, standing back from the animal. "I do lobsters."

Kay put her mouth next to Matt's ear. "Don't worry. Elena said he likes people. You stand here, hold him by his mane, and keep him company. I'll get a bridle from the barn."

Another band of rain raced across the farm. Kay approached the barn, holding on to her jacket's hood and shielding her eyes.

Half of the barn door lay on the ground with a tree limb on top. The other half swung wildly, hanging by one hinge.

Kay found the tack room and picked up a bridle. Passing through the barn entrance, a blast of wind hit the door, crashing it into the back of her head. She fell forward on her stomach, dazed and eyes half-open. She knew she was on the ground, but it was as if she were in that light dozing phase before waking up in the morning—not quite asleep and yet not fully awake, the time when she had her craziest dreams.

Another wind gust caught the damaged door and flung it back with a loud bang. Kay flipped over on her back, the cold rain hitting her in the face. Raising her head, she pushed herself up into a sitting position and touched the lump on the back of her head. "Ouch." She checked her hand. A small spot of blood dotted her palm. She pulled her hood up, tightened the drawstring, and picked up the bridle.

"Where've you been?"

"The barn door hit me in the head."

Matt strained to hear. "The what did what?"

Kay waved him off. "Help me put on the bridle."

With Bramble in his stall, the teens emerged from the barn. Matt wedged a plank against the half of the door remaining to keep it closed and pulled Kay close. "Let's get to the house. It's dangerous out here."

CHAPTER TWENTY-NINE

"**W**e watched from the window," Anna said, helping Kay off with her rain jacket and wet shoes.

Anna walked with her to the bedroom to put on dry clothes. "We saw Matt and the ladder get blown around. Your mom and I were going to come outside and help, but you got things under control."

"Barely," Kay said. "I was scared." With her heart still pounding from the adventure, Kay shuffled into the living room and collapsed on the sofa next to Matt. "I almost let you fall off the ladder."

"No, no. You were great." He gave her a light hug, the first one since he last saw her in Prospect Harbor. "Pretty cool move you made to come on the inside of the ladder and hang on."

"You gave us quite a fright," Kay's mom said, sitting on the other side of her daughter and also giving the teen a much-needed hug. "You both were terrific. But you had my heart racing for a few minutes. What happened with Bramble?" She stroked Kay's hair, pulling out some of the tangles. "There's blood in your hair."

Kay touched the back of her head. "Bramble must've gotten out when the barn doors blew open. Then when I went to get a bridle, the door hit me and knocked me down."

"Are you hurt? Let me see." Elena used both hands and parted Kay's hair. "It's a little cut, and you have a nice bump. I'm sorry you got banged up. Thank you for getting Bramble back in the barn."

Anna returned from the bedroom with two blankets, and tossed one to Matt.

Bobbie took the other and wrapped her daughter in a warm blanket cocoon.

"Internet's *very* slow," Anna said, picking up her phone. "But the phone is still..." She swiped the screen. "Oops. I spoke too soon. No service."

Kay shivered, holding the blanket tight and drawing it up over her mouth, her gaze fixed on the empty footplate of Zack's wheelchair.

Putting her mouth close to Zack's left ear, Elena whispered something and moved to a chair next to Bobbie.

The wind screamed like a high-pitched opera singer while the driving rain raked the side of the house in a near regular rhythm. The hum of the generator became the third instrument in this frightening symphony.

Kay pulled her legs up inside the blanket, wrapped it around her feet, and listened.

CHAPTER THIRTY

Exhausted from working outside in the storm, Kay fought sleep, her eyelids heavy. Each time she opened her eyes, she stared at the bottom of the wheelchair.

"I lost them in Afghanistan." Zack gripped the arms of his wheelchair, shifted his body, and flipped his sweatshirt hood back.

Kay sat up, easing her arms from beneath the blanket. "What? No, I wasn't—"

"It's OK. Everybody stares."

"But—"

"I guess you want to know how I lost them."

"No. I mean, you don't have to tell me. I'm sorry. I've never known anyone who was injured like you—well, until the other day, anyway."

Elena stood and leaned close to Kay's ear. "Please, let him talk. He's never opened up like this to anyone other than me and his friend, Hector."

Anna tugged on Elena's arm. "Was Hector the guy we saw early the other morning?"

"Yes. He comes by sometimes before he goes to work and brings donuts, and they chat. Hector was also on a SEAL team. They met in the hospital."

Kay whispered to Elena, remembering her mom's lecturing that it was rude to do so in front of others, but she didn't know what else to do. "What do I say?"

"You don't have to say anything. Let him talk."

Kay's mom gripped her arm gently. "You, Anna, and Matt stay here and talk. Elena and I will find something for dinner."

Elena pulled back, touching Kay on the shoulder, and walked to the kitchen.

"I guess they don't want to hear my story." Zack gave a hint of a chuckle, breaking through his gloomy expression and his mechanical, monotone voice. He stared at his wrist, rotating three bracelets to line up the names imprinted on each. He stared at Kay. "I know it may not seem that way to you, but I was one of the lucky ones."

CHAPTER THIRTY-ONE

"**M**om, you won't believe what Zack did in the navy in Afghanistan. It's unbelievable."

"I'm sure it's quite extraordinary." Bobbie set a large tray of food it in the middle of the dining table and gave her daughter a big smile. "Navy SEALs are special people."

Anna stood over the tray and plucked a grape. "But he can't tell us everything. It's super secret."

"Top secret," Kay said. "The SEAL teams can't discuss their missions."

Matt inched forward on the couch, his elbows on his knees. "Can't the military help you get artificial legs?"

Zack rubbed his hands together. He glanced at his wife and lowered his head.

Elena knelt next to her husband's wheelchair. "Can I tell them? They'll understand."

He nodded.

"Zack's afraid that—"

"I should tell them," he said, taking a deep breath and touching Elena's arm.

Elena kissed her husband on the cheek and sat in the chair closest to him.

Zack's tone had a sharper edge to it. "People will stare even more with some guy trying to waddle down the street with in those contraptions and using a walking cane. More than when they don't see any legs on my chair's footplates."

"I didn't mean to—"

"It's OK, Matt." Zack's voice rose, but this time the tone was soft and came with a half smile and a nod. "That's the way I feel." His head turned to the side, the Navy SEAL spoke, again in that soft voice. "Maybe it doesn't make sense. But I don't want to endure any more pity or any more stares than I have to."

Anna sniffed and brushed her cheeks with her fingertips. "Excuse me; I need a tissue."

"Bring me one, too, please," Kay said.

Zack sat back in the chair. "Ladies, please. I didn't mean to upset you."

"We're not upset," Anna said. "We're—you know—proud of you, and sorry this happened to you."

He rolled his chair next to the sofa and closer to the girls. "I seemed to have put a damper on our hurricane party."

The one lamp that lit the room flickered and then went off.

Anna gave a shriek through her balled-up fist.

Near blackness filled the room. The only light now came from the candle that Anna had earlier lit and placed on the counter as what she called the "generator backup." But it also had burned near to the bottom of the jar.

"Use your flashlight," Kay said. "It's in your pocket."

Anna squeezed the small flashlight from her jeans pocket. "I thought we had a generator."

Matt scanned the room with his light. "It's probably out of gas. I'll go check."

Five minutes later, Matt stepped into the kitchen. "Let there be light."

"That was quick," Anna said. "You're my hero twice, Matt. First the big tree limb, and now the generator."

"I'm no hero. Zack's the real hero."

"But I mean like Kay was a hero when she almost fell off the bridge trying to help the FBI catch the burglar."

Zack reared his head. "What's this?"

Kay shrugged. "It was nothing, honest."

Leaning forward, Zack twisted his chair around in front of Kay. "I'd like to hear what happened. It sounds exciting."

"I've decided to classify my story as top secret," Kay said. "The government does this with information, so I'm doing it, too."

Anna leaned back and chuckled. "Are you serious? Top secret? Everybody—"

"Dead serious," Kay said, glaring at her friend.

"Kay," Zack said, "I told you some of my story. Please, I'd like to hear yours."

"It's an incredible story," Matt said. "She helped the FBI solve a crime."

"That's something to be proud of," Zack said.

Kay felt the nervous perspiration down the back of her top. "It's kind of a long story."

"That's fine," Zack said. "I'm not running anywhere."

Her mouth drawn tight, Kay bowed her head, avoiding eye contact.

Zack reached out and took her hand. "It's a joke, Kay." He half smiled and nodded. "This is the first time I've ever made a joke about my situation." He swung his head to the right and then let it fall back, his eyes focused on the ceiling. "Yep, the first time. What d'ya know." He leaned forward. "Please tell me this exciting story."

• • •

"Then I went to watch the FBI try and capture the guy, and I thought he was going to get away. I chased him across the bridge, but my bike pedal struck the side of the bridge and flipped me over the rail." Kay swallowed hard. "Then...then I..."

Anna slid a few inches closer to her best friend and slipped her hand in Kay's. "She was hanging on to the rail about a hundred feet above the river." Anna hesitated, catching a glimpse of Kay's face.

Zack leaned on the chair arms. "Then what happened?"

"The man she was chasing heard her screaming and came back to help. He grabbed her by the wrists and yanked her up on the bridge's walkway."

"Did the guy get away?"

Anna squeezed Kay's hand. "The FBI showed up and arrested him."

"Great story, Kay," Zack said. "You *are* a hero."

"Not as great or exciting as your story," Kay said. "And I'm, for sure, not a hero. I did what I thought I had to do, and I gave it all I had."

Zack lowered his head, looking at the bracelets on his wrist. He twisted them, again lining up the names. "That's what heroes do."

CHAPTER THIRTY-TWO

"It's going to be close getting through the night." Matt hung his jacket on a hook beside the door. "There's not much gas left in the can and the generator's using a lot. We should use candles as much as possible. The fridge is the one thing that absolutely needs electricity."

Anna's jaw dropped. "Can't we have a few lights on?"

"Anna, please, enough," Kay said. "You have a flashlight, and we still have a few candles."

"We'll be fine." Bobbie took Anna's hand. "Now, sleeping arrangements. You and Kay can sleep out here on the sofa bed. Elena and Zack can sleep in your bedroom and, Matt, unfortunately that leaves the recliner for you."

"It's perfect. The recliner's better than the cot I've been sleeping on at my aunt's. And if the generator dies, I'll hear it first, and I can restart it."

Bang. Crash. Crunch. Something large and heavy hit the side of the house. Matt cracked the front door open and peeked outside. "It's a huge limb, but not quite as big as the one Kay and I cut down."

A burst of wind and rain slammed against the door, knocking Matt a step backward. With Kay leaning against the door, Matt pushed with his shoulder and closed it.

Bobbie handed him a towel. "What's it like out there?"

"Couldn't see much—only when the lightning flashed. Tree limbs everywhere, and the awning over the Cliffords' back door's gone."

Kay stared at the ceiling. "What's that noise? Sounds like something ripping."

"Roof shingles, most likely," Zack said.

"Are we going to get wet?"

"We'll be OK, unless something knocks a hole in the roof—something pretty big."

"Zack and I are going to bed." Elena glanced at Matt. "I'm going to need some help." She moved behind the wheelchair. "It won't fit through the door. When we stay here in the winter, Zack sleeps on the sofa in the living room. We widened the doorway in the cottage bedroom so the wheelchair could get through. But we didn't have the money to do any more changes. This house and the cottage were built more than a hundred years ago, and they aren't exactly friendly to wheelchairs."

Matt moved next to Elena. "What can I do?"

"Zack'll put his arms over our shoulders, and we'll lift and go sideways through the door."

● ● ●

Elena stood by the bedroom door. "Thanks for helping me with Zack. And thanks for helping us get everything ready for this storm. It's a great relief to know that..." Elena sniffed and touched her finger to the corner of her eye. "Anyway, thanks for being there for me and Zack. We'll see you in the morning."

"Here are some sheets and blankets." Bobbie handed a stack of linens to the three teens. "I'm going to bed, too."

"I don't think I can sleep," Anna said. "The wind and rain are so loud."

Matt switched on the weather radio in the middle of a report: "... with frequent lightning and possible tornadoes. The storm will maintain strength as a category one hurricane until it begins to pass over the Rhode Island and southern Massachusetts coasts. Winds approaching eighty miles per hour can be expected along the immediate coast, and especially on the eastern side of the storm. A state of emergen—"

Kay clicked off the radio.

Anna jerked around, pointing at the radio. "Why did you do that?"

"We know enough. It's bad, and hearing more will only make us nervous and anxious."

"Kay's right," Matt said, spreading a sheet and blanket in the recliner. He covered himself with the blanket, his back to the girls. "We can't do anything except stay inside and be safe."

Anna grabbed the end of the sheet and helped Kay spread it across the bed. "Matt, do you think the generator will last the night?"

"I filled the tank. If we don't use the lights, it should run till first light."

"What if I have to get up and go to the bathroom?"

Kay tossed a pillow at her friend and crawled into the sofa bed. "Use your flashlight and we'll leave a candle burning. Right, Matt?"

No response.

"Matt?"

Anna lay on her back on the bed, whispering to Kay. "I think he's asleep."

Kay snickered. "Or trying to avoid us."

"Why would he avoid us?" Anna grinned and raised her voice. "We're nice people and fun to be around."

Matt's voice projected away from the girls. "Yes, I'm avoiding you. My nieces and nephews woke me at four forty-five this morning. Go to sleep. Good night."

While the occupants of the house on Windcrest Farm slept—or attempted to sleep in the middle of a hurricane—the symphony of noises heard earlier gave way to the roar of marble-sized raindrops spraying the house. It sounded to Kay like freight trains passing by, one after another. The wailing winds became the train's screeching air horn. She pulled the blankets up over her head and covered her ears, waiting for morning.

CHAPTER THIRTY-THREE

Kay bolted upright from a restless slumber and grabbed the flashlight near her pillow. "What was that?" She grabbed her phone and checked the time. "It's only 12:30."

The crackling sound of someone walking on shattered glass echoed throughout the house.

She shined the light at Matt's recliner-bed. "Where's Matt?"

"In here. I'm in the kitchen."

Kay rolled out of bed and slipped on her flip-flops. Stepping into the kitchen, a blast of damp air and a spray of rain in the face slapped her awake.

Anna stuck her head in the kitchen. "What's happening?"

"Something smacked this window—and hard." Matt tiptoed, his shoes crushing the glass strewn across the floor, and his gaze fixed on the gaping hole in the lower half of the window. "We need to find something to cover it."

Elena walked into the kitchen and surveyed the damage. "There're nails, a hammer, and some wood in the generator shed."

"I'll get them." Matt opened the back door and stepped out into the wind. "Push this closed after me." Five minutes later, he banged on the door.

"I'm coming." Kay rotated the handle.

The wind blasted through the doorway. Matt stumbled, knocking Kay down, and spilling his armload of wood over her.

Anna rushed over to Kay. "Are you hurt?"

"I'm fine." Kay pushed aside the splinter-ridden lumber and sat up.

"Sorry about that." Matt gathered the boards. "Let's get this window covered."

Within twenty minutes, Matt, with Kay's help, had covered the window except for one last plank. The wind poured through that narrow opening. Kay's arms ached from holding it in place. Matt held the nail between his fingers and reached for the hammer. Like a giant hand, the wind pushed on the plank. Kay lost her grip, and the narrow piece of wood flew back, slapping Matt in the side of his head.

The teens grabbed the plank, each holding an end, and approached the opening again.

Matt laid the hammer on the counter. "That does it. Let's tack this plastic sheet over the window."

Kay stepped back. "We do good work."

Elena swept the last of the broken glass. "Nice job. Thank you both...*again*. I hope nothing else happens."

Anna shined her light on the patched window. "I agree. Very nice work." She walked back to the sofa bed and hopped in.

Kay patted her arms and face with a towel and slid beneath the covers. She rolled over on her side and faced the recliner. "Will our patch hold?"

"I'm sure it will." Matt angled his head toward the sofa, held the flashlight to his face, and winked at Kay. "We make a great team."

Kay grinned, pulled the sheet up around her neck, and closed her eyes.

CHAPTER THIRTY-FOUR

S livers of light slipped between the planks of the boarded-up kitchen window.

Her eyes half open, Kay rolled over, squinted at the window, and faced the recliner.

"Good morning," Matt said, looking straight at her. "I think we made it."

Kay blinked and forced her eyes wide. "Morning? I feel like I never went to sleep last night. What time is it?"

Matt checked his watch. "It's five forty-nine." He sat up and put on his boots.

Anna reached for the blanket and tucked it around her neck. "It's too early to be awake."

"Listen." Kay swung her legs off the side of the bed.

"I don't hear anything," Anna said.

"That's the point. No wind or rain, and the sun's shining."

Matt opened the front door. "You have to see this."

"What is it?" Kay slipped on her sneakers and ran to the door. Standing next to Matt, she shielded her eyes from the sun. "Look at that blue sky. Quite a change from yesterday." Her gaze shifted to the scene by the house. Broken tree limbs and green leaves littered the porch. Mixed with the limbs and twigs, aluminum sheeting from the awning lay scattered across the yard. "That awning looks like it went through a giant paper shredder."

"What a mess." Anna sat on the top step of the stairs, put on her shoes, and met up with her friends walking through the yard.

Kay's mom poked her head out the door. "Be careful. We'll find something for breakfast. And, Matt, I think the generator died."

After getting the generator humming again, Matt caught up with Kay and Anna, walking toward the land where the house was being built. "Where are you going?"

Kay pointed. "Some huge trees blew over down near the river. They fell over some of the stone walls."

The three walked up to one of the damaged walls closer to the river and fifty yards from the construction site. A huge, uprooted elm tree lay across the scattered rocks.

"It'll take a long time to fix this one," Anna said.

Hands on her hips, Kay stared at the gray line of stone walls. "They won't be too upset seeing these knocked down. More than likely, the walls will be torn down anyway to build more houses." She nudged a few of the stones and knelt beside one. "Look. There's writing or a drawing on this rock."

Anna moved next to Kay. "Maybe some kids did these a long time ago." Anna bent down and flipped over a stone. "Nothing here."

Matt stepped over the stones, nudging some with his foot. "Here's one." He picked it up and moved from the shade into the sunlight. "It's definitely a sketch of something."

Within a few minutes, the teens had discovered eighteen of the stones with drawings on them. They laid them in an area away from the fallen wall.

Clasping her hands behind her neck, Kay stepped back from the array. "That's it."

Anna stood next to Kay, surveying the find. "What's *it?*"

Kay gave her best friend a hug—a real one, not a 'Kay hug'—and grabbed Matt, pinning his arms to his side. She gave him a quick kiss on the cheek and jumped back. "Sorry."

Turning away, Kay's face glowed. Why did she do that?

"If you're through kissing Matt," Anna said, spinning her friend around, "would you please tell me what you meant by 'that's it.'"

Kay gave Anna the bug-eyed, you're-embarrassing-me look.

Anna gave Kay a full-toothed grin in return.

"What I mean is, this is how we stop the construction," Kay said. "This place has got to be a significant archeological site."

Matt and Anna looked at each other, then at Kay.

"What? It could be."

"It's not that," Matt said. "It's that phrase 'significant archeological site.' Where did you get that?"

"I found some stuff online about places around Rhode Island and Massachusetts where people have found Indian artifacts."

Anna pivoted to look back up the low hill at the basement pit where she and Kay had gone for their unplanned swim. "That means they won't be able to build here in this spot."

"I'm hoping this whole area can be made into a historical site, and Mr. McCallum will have to stop building the houses."

Anna stared back at the construction site. "All of them?"

"I hope so," Kay said. "Is something wrong?"

"No. Nothing's wrong. I was…No. I guess it's a good thing if they stop all the building."

"I'm glad you agree," Kay said, tilting her head at her friend. She turned and focused on the stones they'd found, circling them in short steps.

"What are you staring at?" Anna moved beside Kay. "Find something?"

"Maybe these are stones that were part of a bigger drawing."

Matt pulled out his phone. "Could be. Let's take some photos. Both of you move to the other side of the rocks." He snapped a picture while standing and then knelt and took close-ups.

Kay gave him a thumbs-up. "This was a great idea, Matt. Send those to me, please. I want to do some research."

"Will do." Matt shoved his phone in his pocket and moved next to Kay. "Remember, you told me your dad said not to feel bad if you get stonewalled trying to help Elena."

"Yes, I do. Maybe the stone wall's going to help me for a change, and it might come tumbling down on somebody."

CHAPTER THIRTY-FIVE

Kay yanked the screen door open. "We found it."

Bobbie sat with Zack and Elena around the dining room table. "What did you find?"

"Show them the pictures, Matt."

Elena took the phone from Matt. "Looks like a tree blew over and knocked down a section of the stone wall."

Kay reached in and swiped with her finger. "Keep going. You'll see."

Bobbie craned her neck to view the screen. "Are those drawings on the rocks?"

Elena's jaw dropped. "This is amazing. And you found these on the Calder parcel?"

Kay beamed. "That's right. This is the kind of thing Anna and I were searching for when we fell in that basement pit at the construction site. We found a bunch of these. There could be more."

Elena handed the phone to Matt. "I have a friend at a university who can help identify these," she said.

"And I know someone who can help us, too." Kay nodded at Matt. "Bolles?"

"Why not? I'll send him the pictures and see what he says."

Anna stood in the bedroom doorway, tapped on the wall switch, and pointed at the ceiling light. "Look, everybody. The electricity's back on!"

CHAPTER THIRTY-SIX

Hank held on to the surfboard and ducked his head beneath the umbrella. "Mrs. Telfair, my mom's coming down in a few minutes. She dropped me off and went back to the house for something. I told her you'd be here. She might come by to meet you."

"That would be nice, Hank," Bobbie said, plopping down in her chair. "I'd like to meet her, too."

"I told her watch for your silver umbrella and your big red beach bag." He pointed at Anna. "Ready for another lesson?"

"Be careful," Bobbie said. "It's only been two days since the hurricane. The sign at the lifeguard stand said there's a good possibility of rip currents, and there're some big waves rolling in."

"Don't worry, Mrs. Telfair. If it's too rough, I won't let her try it today."

"I'll be careful." Anna zipped up her wetsuit and stuffed her shorts and top in her bag.

"You have matching black wetsuits," Kay said. "How cute. You're twins."

"They look like professional surfers," Kay's mom said.

"Thank you Mrs. Telfair." Anna stuck her tongue out at Kay and followed Hank thirty yards down the beach to the surfers' area. Hank dropped his board into the water and helped Anna climb on. He waded alongside, helping her paddle.

"The water's rough even for an excellent swimmer," Kay said. "Anna's basically a pool splasher."

"That's not a very nice thing to say," Bobbie said.

"Look at her, Mom. She's having trouble getting through the waves."

Bobbie sat forward in her chair. "She is struggling a bit trying to stand on the board."

"That wave broke over her head," Kay said. "It knocked her off the board. Ouch. That had to hurt."

A shadow fell across Bobbie's lap. "Hi. You must be Anna's mom." The woman stood at the edge of the umbrella and pointed toward the surfers. "Hank's my son."

"No," Bobbie said. "Actually, Anna's a friend of my daughter, Kay."

"Oops, sorry—I knew that. A momentary lapse."

"I'm Bobbie, and this is Kay."

The woman shook Bobbie's hand. "I'm Kris." She extended her hand to Kay. "Hank and Anna have told me a lot about you."

Kay put on the polite smile, no dimples, only a slight lift in the corners of her mouth, all to hide that fact she was annoyed. Did Anna mention the bridge escapade? The Maine adventure? What exactly did she tell Hank's mom?

"We'd love to have you sit with us," Bobbie said.

"Thanks." Kris unfolded her chair. "Hank said you moved to New Jersey from Florida last year. I love Florida."

"So do *I*," Kay said.

Bobbie gave Kay the "be nice" look, combining a glare and a plea. "It was a tough transition—Kay changing schools and all that."

"I know what you mean. We moved here from Boston a few years ago. It was tough for Hank at first. But we're close to the beach, and the summers are great. And fall and spring are the best, in my opinion."

"I remember winters growing up in Rhode Island and my dad breaking out the snowblower," Bobbie said. "And then we had to make up the school days we missed in the winter during our summer break."

"Winter's not too bad," Kris said. "Actually better than Boston. I think it's because I don't have to drive on icy roads in heavy traffic. Anna said you're in Little Compton for a month. Where are you staying?"

"We're renting a house over at Windcrest Farm," Bobbie said.

Kris's expression changed from a warm smile to a startled look. She looked away and coughed. "Excuse me." The woman took out a water bottle and drank.

Bobbie shot a puzzled glance at her daughter, and Kay returned the same look.

Bobbie turned to Kris. "Do you know the place?"

"What...yes...I..." Kris put the bottle to her lips and swallowed. "Sometimes I buy flowers from the roadside stand."

"They're beautiful flowers, aren't they," Bobbie said.

"Very nice," Kris said. "In fact, I..."

A female lifeguard ran past, trailed by two young men.

"Wow. They're in a hurry," Bobbie said. "They can't be more than seventeen or eighteen. And they get younger every year. Or maybe it's because I'm getting older."

Kay pushed herself up from her low beach chair and stepped from beneath the umbrella. She jogged a few yards and yelled back to the two moms. "They're helping someone out of the water. I don't see Anna." Running toward the beachgoers gathered in the shallows, she high-stepped into the water. Between breaks in the curtain of bystanders around the lifeguards, Kay caught a glimpse of someone in a black wetsuit being carried to shore. Was it Anna? She cupped her hands at her mouth. "Anna! Anna! Where are you?"

"I'm here," Anna said, picking her way through the crowd of bystanders. She took in three quick, deep breaths. "I'm OK."

Kay grabbed her and gave her a hug. "I couldn't see at first, and I thought it was you the lifeguards were carrying."

Anna trembled, wrapping her arms around herself. "It's Hank."

Kay released her friend from the embrace and then grabbed her again. "You scared me. Is he OK?"

"I think he'll be OK, but he got a nasty bang on the head. He got knocked off his board, and then the board came down on him."

The crowd moved with the lifeguards, who walked with Hank out of the water and up onto the beach.

Bobbie and Kris ran up behind the girls. "What's happening?"

"It's Hank," Anna said. "The board hit him in the head."

Kris pushed through the crowd, and stood by the lifeguards, hovering over her son.

"I'll go stand with Kris," Bobbie said to Kay. "You take Anna and sit her down."

Anna collapsed in the chair. "He was showing me..." She swallowed and took in a deep breath, holding back the tears. "Showing me how to turn around on the board, when a huge wave hit us. I went under, and when I came up I saw the board in the air. It landed on his head."

"You stay." Kay wrapped a towel around Anna. "I want to see what's happening."

Kay walked up behind her mom. "How is he?"

"He's going to be all right. He's sitting up. I heard him say the hit dazed him for a few seconds. I'm going back to sit with Anna. We shouldn't leave her alone."

Kay inched closer to the group and stood behind Hank's mom.

"You've got a small cut, but you should be fine," the female lifeguard said, opening a small adhesive bandage and putting it on Hank's head.

One of the male lifeguards knelt beside the boy. "What's your name?"

Kris answered for her son. "His name is Hank—Henry McCallum Jr."

Kay took a step back, her eyes fixed on the young teen on the ground, and her mouth wide open. She twisted around and looked back at her best friend, sitting under the umbrella. "She must've known. Why didn't she tell me?"

CHAPTER THIRTY-SEVEN

Anna flung her beach towel over the clothesline in the backyard of the rental house. "I didn't know until I heard you tell Matt about Mr. McCallum coming to the house. I asked Hank about it and he said, yes, that his dad was in charge of building the houses near Elena's farm."

Kay put a clothespin on the beach towel and glared at Anna. "Why didn't you tell me?"

"I was worried I would upset you."

"All this time you pretended to approve of what we're doing to stop the houses from being built?"

"I was also afraid you'd tell your mom, and then she wouldn't let me hang out with Hank."

Kay stomped toward the house.

"Kay, wait." Anna chased her inside and sat on the bed next to her friend.

Kay jerked her head to the right. "You thought my mom would stop you? She's not like that."

"How would I know that? And besides, you're my best friend, and I didn't want to do anything to hurt you or make you mad at me."

"Angry Kay" became "surprised Kay"—and then "speechless Kay." She didn't know how to react. Anna, her best friend, was friends with the enemy's son—the enemy being Henry McCallum.

"Are you mad at me?"

"No. I'm not mad. I'm disappointed. No, not disappointed, I'm..." Kay folded her arms. "I don't know what I am. I know you like Hank, and—"

"I do. He's nice, and he thinks a lot of you and Matt. He says you make a great couple."

"Thanks." Kay pulled her legs up on the bed and folded her arms. "You and Hank are good together, too."

"He's made a surfer out of me. I never thought I would be able to do that."

"Yeah. I've seen you surf. Your feet are shuffling around so fast it's like you're dancing on hot rocks when you try and stand on the board."

Anna pursed her lips in a fake anger expression. "I do not."

"Do, too."

"Do not."

"Do, too." Kay made a fist and soft-punched her friend in the arm.

"Ow. That hurt."

"Baby."

Anna half smiled and shook her head. "You're impossible."

Twenty seconds passed in silence.

Anna sat forward to face Kay. "Hank's parents are going through some bad times. His mom told me his dad lost his job a few years ago. That's why they moved to Rhode Island. If you and Elena stop the construction, he could lose his job again. Are you going to keep trying to stop the houses from being built?"

Kay stared straight ahead.

"Answer me, please. Are you?"

Taking a deep breath, Kay lowered her head slightly. "Yes. I am."

CHAPTER THIRTY-EIGHT

Kay's fingers skimmed across her laptop's touchpad. "Mom, look. I found a web site that has lots of information and pictures of drawings made by Native Americans in New England. Check this out."

"Interesting." Bobbie sat in a chair next to Kay. "Where is this?"

"It's in Taunton, Massachusetts. It's called Dighton Rock, and it's in a museum at Dighton Rock State Park. The rock has these drawings called petroglyphs. Some people think the Wampanoags made them. I learned that the Sakonnets who lived around here were part of the Wampanoag tribe. Some of these petroglyphs are a little like the ones we found on the rocks."

Elena knocked on the screen door. "May I come in?"

"Sure," Bobbie said. "What's up?"

"I was picking up some limbs from the storm, and I saw this front-end loader down near the stone wall that fell over. They're digging up what's left of it and putting it in a dump truck."

Kay jumped up from her chair. "What? They can't do that. Is that legal?"

"Legal or not, they're doing it," Elena said. "Do you want to go down there with me?"

Kay pushed back from the table and stood. "Of course. I want to know what's going on."

"Anna's taking a nap," Bobbie said. "I should stay here. I wouldn't want her to wake up and find out we're all gone. Be careful. You'll both be trespassing."

Kay and Elena crossed the open field, climbed over one stone wall, and walked up to the front-end loader moving the rocks. The man in the driver's seat jerked his head to the left to see them and then jerked it back to the right and idled the engine. "Can I help you ladies?"

Elena stepped close and raised her voice over the noisy equipment. "You're not building a house on this spot now. Why are you destroying this wall?"

"I was told to move it and take the stone down to a beach area to help stop erosion."

"Who asked you to do it?"

"I assume the landowners—or one of them, anyway."

Kay inched closer to Elena and glared at the man. "Was it Mr. McCallum?"

"Don't know the man."

Kay pointed behind her. "He's building the house up on the hill."

"Sorry. Name doesn't ring a bell. But I have a work order. His name must be on that; otherwise my boss wouldn't have sent me down here. I work for a landscaping company. My company doesn't build houses." He hopped off the machine, went to the cab of the dump truck, and pulled out a clipboard. "Here it is. It's signed by a..." The man lifted his glasses off his nose. "It's hard to read the signature. Could be Boller or—"

Kay's jaw dropped as if someone had hung a weight on it. "Bolles?"

"That's it," the man said. "Yep. That's an *S*. B-O-L-L-E-*S*."

"Who?" Elena turned to Kay.

"Hanscomb Bolles." Kay shook her head, surveying the destroyed stone wall. "I don't understand. Bolles is the man I sent the pictures to—the professor Matt and I met at the restaurant the other day. Why would he be paying to have these rocks moved?"

Turning on her heels, Kay stormed back to the house. Every few steps, she pounded the heels of her sneakers into the ground, angry at what she saw at the wall. Her face red from the heat, she stepped through the front door.

Elena entered a few seconds behind her and breathing hard. "Girl, you're a fast walker."

Kay opened the fridge door. "I'll get us some water."

"I'll fix you both a glass," Bobbie said. "Sit and rest."

Anna eased into the kitchen. "Your mom told me what happened. Was it Hank's dad?"

"No," Elena said. "It was the man Kay sent the photos to. He told the landscape company to move the rocks."

Bobbie handed Elena and Kay each a glass. "Not the history professor you met at the restaurant?"

Kay gulped down the cold liquid and coughed. "That's him, but I don't understand what's going on here."

The sound of a vehicle's engine echoed from the driveway.

Bobbie looked out the window. "It's Matt."

Running to the door, Kay met her friend with a sixty-mile-an-hour rush of words. "You won't believe this. They're digging up the stone walls where we found the drawings, and they're dumping the rocks at the beach somewhere—and Hanscomb Bolles told them to do it."

"Whoa. What's this about?"

Elena jumped in. "They're tearing down the rest of the wall and hauling it off."

Kay threw her hands in the air. "That's our proof that this is an archeogi...archeolegic...I'm so upset I can't even say it. The photos you took are all the evidence we have."

"Not quite." Matt grinned and motioned to the group. "Come with me."

Kay, her mom, Anna, and Elena followed Matt out the door and over to his truck.

The young teen lifted the cover on the bed of his pickup. "Here you are."

CHAPTER THIRTY-NINE

Kay peered into the truck bed. "When did you get the rocks?"
"I drove down to the wall after I left you and picked them up. Helps to have a four-wheel drive vehicle. I was going to stop and tell you, but I was supposed to babysit for my aunt and I was running late. Then I decided to surprise you."

Elena stared at the rocks. "You did surprise us."

"I thought they might get covered up if the construction started down in that area. I didn't know where the next house would be built."

Standing on the truck bumper, Anna counted the rocks. "There're only eight."

"I didn't want to stay too long in case somebody showed up. This is all I had time to pick up." Matt pointed to the bicep on his left arm. "Also, I'm pretty strong, but those things must weigh forty pounds each."

"Thank you, thank you." Elena hugged the teen. "There's hope yet."

"I need to give you a hug, too." Kay wrapped her arms around Matt and squeezed him.

He faked a cough. "Ouch. You're strong. I should have had you help me load those rocks." Gently pinching her upper arm, he presented a wide grin. "You've got muscles. What do you think, Anna?"

With a blank expression, Anna said, "Yeah, sure. She's strong." She stepped back from the truck and walked into the house.

"Did I say something?"

Kay pursed her lips. "You remember Hank—the guy teaching her to surf—his dad is the builder. If we stop the construction, his dad could lose his job."

"That's a shock. Is she mad at you?"

"No, we're OK. Anna agrees with us that the houses will spoil the view and take up good farmland. But she's afraid that if we find a way to stop the construction, Hank's dad will get fired."

"I would hate for him to lose his job, but I also don't want to lose my farm." Elena reached into the truck bed and wiped the dirt from one of the stones. "I think we have a chance of stopping the houses. I sent Matt's photos to an anthropologist I know at Dartmouth and she says these drawings could be one of the best examples of Native American petroglyphs ever found in New England."

Kay leaned into the truck bed to get another look at the rocks. "What's an anthropologist? I thought you'd send the photos to an archeologist."

"Like you and Anna wanted to be." Matt laughed. "Instead, you both became mud wrestlers."

"Very funny." Kay gave a fake sneer.

"To answer your question, Kay, an anthropologist studies every area of what humans do. Archeology studies the physical evidence. The anthropologist gave me the name of an attorney who does a lot of work with land issues and archeological sites. I have an appointment with the attorney the day after tomorrow. Anyone want to come with me?"

CHAPTER FORTY

Elena pushed open the door and walked over to a young man at a desk. "We're here to see Ms. Hammonds. I'm Elena Clifford."

"Thanks for letting us come with you," Kay said, standing beside Elena.

"I hope having you and Matt here will help me, since you're the ones who found the rock drawings."

The man rose, waved his arm, and led the trio into a spacious office with oak-paneled walls, an enormous leather sofa, and a huge mahogany desk. Behind the desk sat fifty-five-year-old Harriet Hammonds, one of New England's best attorneys, well known for her work helping to save historic lands and buildings. Hammonds rose and straightened her gray suit jacket. "Mrs. Clifford, nice to meet you in person."

Elena introduced Kay and Matt. The three moved to the sofa, with Hammonds sitting across from them.

"Professor Trask at Dartmouth told me about your situation and sent me the photos."

Kay put her hands together in a praying position and tapped her fingers against each other. "Can we stop the construction? Please tell me we can."

Elena looked at Kay, gave a weak smile, and then turned to Hammonds. "We're very anxious to know."

"Unfortunately it's not that simple. My experts examined the photos and also did some very quick research on the property. The rock drawings appear to be of Native American origin, probably from the 1600s or earlier."

Kay sat forward. "That's good, right?"

"Yes, that is good, but..." Hammonds took off her glasses and took in a deep breath, exhaling with her lips close together in a quiet rush of air.

Kay slid back a few inches. Was this the signal for bad news to come?

Looking back at Kay, Elena then turned to Hammonds. "But what?"

"We can't prove exactly where the rocks were found."

"But the photos," Matt said. "And we have eight of the rocks."

"The photos do show Kay and the other girl standing with the rocks and next to a partially destroyed stone wall," Hammonds said. "But, there are untold miles of stone walls scattered across New England. Any good attorney could argue that the photos were taken at some other location."

"So that's it?" Kay stood. "We can't stop the construction?"

"You can pay me or some other law firm to plead your case with the appropriate government agencies, but the landowners would bring in their attorneys and fight it tooth and nail. Obviously, if the land were to be declared a major archeological or historical site, they'd have to stop building."

Kay eased back down on the massive sofa. "How much would that cost?"

Elena patted her on the arm. "It's over. I don't have the money for an attorney." She nodded toward Matt. "Thank you both for trying."

Nothing was said during the first twenty minutes of the ride in Matt's truck from Providence to Little Compton, until Kay broke the silence. "What will you do now?"

"Pray that people will want to stay at Windcrest without that expansive view of the river." Elena glanced out the window. "But I doubt they will. I'll have to find more music students or get a full-time teaching job. And that won't be easy. Zack has a tough time when I leave him for long periods."

A somber mood remained for the rest of the drive to Windcrest.

"Thank you for driving, Matt. And thanks to you both—again—for trying to help me and Zack." She gave them each a hug and walked to the cottage.

Kay eased her hand into Matt's. "Do you want to stay for dinner?"

"Thanks, but I need to get back to my aunt's. I told her I would babysit. My aunt and uncle are having a date night."

Kay caught a glimpse of Anna standing on the small porch and turned to Matt. "Call me tomorrow."

Seconds after Matt's truck rolled onto the pavement, Anna ran down the steps to Kay. "Hank's dad lost his job. What did you do?"

CHAPTER FORTY-ONE

"**C**alm down." Kay dropped her purse on the table. "Where's my mom?"

"She's gone to the store."

"Now, what's going on with Hank's dad?"

"Your mom and I went to the beach so I could surf with Hank, and he didn't seem too happy to see me. I thought it was something I did. I asked him what was wrong, but he wouldn't tell me. When I got home, he texted me and apologized, and that's when he told me his dad wasn't working for the construction company anymore."

"But that doesn't mean he got fired," Kay said. "Maybe he got laid off. Or maybe he quit."

"Why would he quit? I told you he lost his job in Boston. That's why they moved here."

Kay stepped back, reeling from Anna's shrill tone. "There's got to be more to this."

"Hank said his dad isn't working at that company, the…" Anna checked her messages. "The HB Development Corporation." She looked up. "They might have to move again. Hank said his dad was looking into engineering jobs in Ohio."

Kay told her about their visit to the attorney in Providence. "That's all we did. I'm sorry that Hank's dad lost his job, but I had nothing to do with it."

"That may be true, but something happened to make him lose his job," Anna said, wiping away a tear. "And you and Elena and Matt have been trying to do everything you can to stop the houses from being built."

"You're not listening, Anna." Kay put her hands on Anna's shoulders. "We didn't do anything."

"Hank and I were getting along so well." Anna struggled for a deep breath between sobs. "And I was hoping since Rhode Island is not that far from New Jersey, that maybe—"

"You're getting way ahead of yourself, Anna. Let's think this through. What exactly did you tell Hank?"

"I told him that we found these rocks with the drawings and things on them. I said you were going to send the photos to someone to find out more about them."

Scratching her head, Kay sat at the table. "Was he angry when you told him what we were trying to do?"

"Not exactly. I couldn't figure out what he was thinking. But he acted like he knew something."

"Would Hank talk to me?"

"I don't know. He's at the beach. He's teaching a middle-school kid how to surf."

"Would you bike with me down to the beach?"

"Sure, I'll go with you," Anna said. "Maybe he'll talk to you."

CHAPTER FORTY-TWO

Standing with Kay at the water's edge, Anna waved at Hank. He waved his arm above his head, caught a wave, and rode his board to within a few yards of the girls. "I don't see any suits." He picked up his board and winked at Anna. "You guys come here just to see me?"

Kay stepped forward. "Hank, can we talk?"

"Sure. Let's sit here." He spread the towel on the sand, switching his gaze from one girl to the other. "What's going on? You both have that serious look."

"I understand your dad is no longer with the company building the houses," Kay said.

Hank nodded and shot a glance at Anna. "That's right."

"I don't mean to get personal, but I need to know: How did he leave the company? Did he quit?"

"You're right. It is personal." The young boy hesitated. "But, yes, he quit."

Anna reared her head back. "I thought you said he—"

"I told you he was no longer with the company. I didn't want to give out any more information. Since we'd been talking about maybe seeing each other after the summer, I was trying to let you know that I might be moving away."

Kay asked her burning question. "OK, why *did* he quit?"

"I'm not sure he wants people to know." Hank drew swirls in the sand with his finger. "Besides, I'm not supposed to know. I overheard my mom and dad talking."

Kay got up on her knees on the blanket and sat back on her heels. "Anna thinks that finding the rocks with the drawings had something to do with your dad leaving his job."

The boy looked at Anna and turned to Kay. "It did."

Kay slumped back on the towel and shook her head. "What? How? Elena's lawyer said we wouldn't have much chance of stopping the construction. The rocks that Matt saved and the photos didn't help."

"The construction *hasn't* stopped," Hank said.

Kay took a deep breath and exhaled with a swooshing sound, her cheeks expanding like small balloons. "I'm completely confused. Please tell me what happened with your dad. I promise I won't tell anyone."

Hank hesitated, staring out at the rolling surf.

Anna touched Hank's arm. "I promise, too. We won't repeat a word of it."

"OK. Here's the story. My dad saw the photos of the rocks at his office in Fall River."

"This doesn't make sense," Anna said. "How was he able to see them at his office?"

Kay threw up her hands, palms out. "*I* know. The name of the company is HB Development. H-B—Hanscomb Bolles."

Hank's eyes widened. "You know Mr. Bolles?"

Anna threw her hands up. "Who is Mr. Bolles?"

"He owns the company my dad works for."

"Matt and I met Professor Bolles at the restaurant."

Anna wrinkled her brow. "That's the professor you said you sent the photos to?"

"Yes. He heard Matt and me talking about wanting to find something that proved the Sakonnets lived on that land. He said he would help us if we needed it. He's also the man who told the landscaping company to move the rocks we found. It all makes sense now." Kay shifted her body to sit flat on the towel. "But that still doesn't tell us why your dad quit his job. What do the photos have to do with it?"

"My dad saw them on Mr. Bolles's desk. Bolles said they weren't important. After Bolles left, Dad took a closer look and saw that they were taken at the property where he's working on the house. He asked about the pictures the next day, and he told Bolles that he knew where they were taken."

Anna chimed in. "But he couldn't let it go, right?"

"My dad's pretty passionate about his work, and he can't stand it if something's not right. Maybe that comes from being an engineer."

Anna lowered her head at Kay, peering over her sunglasses. "I know someone else who's like that—someone who can't let things go."

Kay shook her head at her friend and focused on Hank. "What else did your dad say to Bolles?"

"He wanted to know if they were going to build in the area where you found the rock drawings. Bolles told him it didn't matter, because all those stone walls would be gone soon. Dad said he could build around the walls and save them. Bolles said that if they didn't get rid of the walls they couldn't build as many houses. He said it was none of my dad's business, and that my dad's job was to get the houses built."

Anna raised her eyebrows and lowered her head at Hank. "So your dad quit?"

"Yes. The next day."

"Your dad must care a lot about protecting historic sites to give up his job," Kay said.

"He does care, and I think what Mr. Bolles said to my dad about building where you found the rock drawings made him angry." Hank twisted the surfboard leash around his hand. "There's also another reason for him leaving. My dad thought the company was having money troubles."

"Maybe that's why not much work has been done on the site since they dug the basement," Kay said.

"Thanks for telling us, Hank," Anna said. She turned to Kay. "I'm sorry I blamed you. I had it all wrong. Forgive me?"

Kay's eyes had that hundred-yard stare—a view into nowhere.

"Kay, did you hear me?"

"Yeah, sure. Of course, I forgive you."

Anna gave her a gentle tap-tap on the head. "Hello, Kay. Where are you?"

"I'm thinking.

"Oh, no."

Hank shifted his gaze from Kay back to Anna. "What do you mean, 'oh, no'?"

"When Kay thinks this hard, it usually means one thing—trouble."

"Trouble for her?"

"Trouble for everybody."

CHAPTER FORTY-THREE

Kay sat at the dining table with her mom, Matt, and Elena, listening to the phone conversation between Elena and attorney Harriet Hammonds. "Thank, Mrs. Hammonds. Yes, I will."

Kay spread her arms on the table. "What did the attorney say about Hank's dad being a witness?"

"She said that even if he recognized the location of the wall from the photos, that wouldn't be enough evidence to take to a government agency or to use in court."

Kay slumped in her chair. "It's like my dad said, we were stonewalled at every turn."

"Ironic and sad at the same time," Elena said.

Returning from the kitchen with a cup of tea, Anna pulled up a chair. "From the expressions on your faces, I'd say it wasn't good news from the lawyer."

Elena tilted her head back. "Nope, not at all."

"Hank's dad said the company had money troubles," Anna said. "If they have no more money, maybe they'll stop building."

"Wishful thinking, I'm afraid," Elena said.

Bobbie slid her chair back. "We may be sad, but we still have to eat dinner. Who's up for some hot dogs and beans?"

"Not for me, thanks," Elena said. "Maybe it's been wishful thinking from the beginning." She pushed back from the table. "Thank you, Kay. And thank you all for everything. I'm sorry things didn't work out—sorry for us all." Standing with the screen door ajar, she waved. "See you later."

"I feel so bad for her," Anna said.

Matt nodded. "Yep, it is sad."

Kay stood. "You all sound like you're giving up."

"We didn't give up," Anna said. "Remember? We got stonewalled. Stone is hard. You can't go through it. It's impossible."

Bobbie yelled from the kitchen. "Anna, do you really believe that? How long have you known my daughter?"

"Mom!"

CHAPTER FORTY-FOUR

"This is almost as bad as riding in Matt's truck." Kay squeezed the brake levers hard. She snatched the handlebars, first to the left, and then to the right, dodging a deep rut. "I didn't think it would take us this long."

"So far, twenty minutes." Anna stole a glance at her watch and almost veered into the brush and weeds. "You said it was a ten-minute ride in the truck."

"Stop worrying. We're almost to Mr. Calder's house. And watch where you're going."

Anna braked hard to avoid hitting Kay. "Did you leave a note for your mom?"

"No. We'll be home by the time she gets back from the market."

Anna shook her head and pedaled up beside Kay. "Do you think Mr. Calder will listen to you?"

"We won't know until we ask, and I need to know. He did say he regretted selling the land."

"The door's closed." Anna rolled up to the house behind Kay. "Maybe he's not—"

"I'm here." Calder stepped from behind a tall shrub at the side of the house, shears in hand. "Trying to keep the place from turning into a jungle." He laid the shears down. "Didn't expect to see you here. But you're welcome anyway. And who's this young lady?"

"This is my friend, Anna."

"Hello, Anna. Nice to meet you." Calder dropped the shears, picked up his baseball bat cane, and walked toward the stairs. He stopped to bang on his left leg. "I've got to get this fixed."

Anna's eyes widened. She tugged at Kay's arm.

Kay whispered, tilting her head at Anna. "Don't worry. He's very nice. Trust me."

"And where's the young man who was with you the last time?"

Kay stood her bike next to the stair railing. "He's babysitting."

Calder laughed. "Interesting."

"That's not his real job," Anna said. "He's staying with his aunt and uncle in Tiverton; and he's—"

"Come inside and have a seat, young ladies."

The girls sat on the sofa with the mismatched cushions. Anna sat on a section and sank in. She grabbed Kay's arm and pulled herself up to the edge of the cushion.

"Sorry about the sofa cushions. Been meaning to get new ones," Calder said. "And I'm sorry I don't have any refreshments to offer you. I didn't get to the store this week. My old pickup's kind of sick. Needs some T-L-C." He pulled up his right pant leg and pointed. "Also had a leg problem. Had to jury-rig the thing until I can get to the veterans hospital."

Anna recoiled, sinking back into the soft cushion, and bumping the wooden-slatted back.

Calder covered his leg. "My apologies, young lady. Thought maybe your friends had told you about my mechanical legs." He tapped the left one. "Got two of 'em."

Anna swallowed hard. "No, they didn't tell me. I've never seen them. But I met this guy, Zack, last week. He lost his legs in Afghanistan and—"

Kay touched Anna on the arm and turned toward Calder. She told him about the rock drawings, Hank's dad and Bolles, and the talks with the attorney.

"*That's* what Bolles wanted. That scoundrel." Calder nodded. "I'm sorry to hear you couldn't find a way to stop the building on that beautiful piece of land." He shook his head and looked at the two teens. "But you didn't come way out here just to tell me about Bolles, did you?"

"No, Mr. Calder," Kay said. "We have a favor to ask."

Calder sat up straight in his chair. His left leg clicked and, again, Anna flinched.

"We wanted to ask you if you would buy back the property you sold to Bolles's company."

Calder rubbed his balding head. "I didn't even know it was Bolles who bought the property. It was a bunch of lawyers and real estate people who contacted me. All I knew was that a corporation had bought the property." He picked up a framed photo on the table next to him—a photo that Kay had seen before and assumed it was Calder and his wife on their wedding day. "Is the land for sale?" His mouth twitched from side to side as if trying to scratch his beard without touching it. "You did say that someone is building homes on the property."

"So far, the hole for a basement for one house is all they've done," Anna said.

"The developer might be going bankrupt," Kay said. "You could buy the land back—maybe for less than they paid you for it. You said you never touched the money and—"

"I don't have to make money off the deal," Calder said. "I don't have many needs, especially now that my wife is gone. And why would I need that land?"

Kay jutted her head forward. "You said you regretted selling the land, didn't you?"

"I did say that." He shot a glance at the picture. "My wife and I were going to build a small house and barn on that piece of property after I retired, but she got sick and things changed. Besides, the lawyers spent months getting me to sell the land and then setting up the deal. I don't think I want to go through that again. Too many papers to sign, and most of 'em I didn't read. I trusted the lawyers." Calder took in a deep breath and gave a long, slow exhale. "Not sure if I did the right thing. Anyway, it's done."

Pressing her lips together, Kay's face showed dejection and then resignation. Stonewalled again—and probably for the last time—trying to save the view and the stone walls for Elena and Zack and all their future renters at Windcrest Farm. This was it, her last shred of hope gone.

"Young lady, I'm sorry things didn't work out the way you wanted them to. And I understand your passion and energy. I used to be like that—a long time ago."

Kay glanced at Anna. She wanted to cry, but not here. Not in front of another war hero. She'd done that already in front of Zack. "Sorry to have bothered you, Mr. Calder."

"No bother. Next time call me. Make sure I'm home. I might have my truck running again. And I do have a cell phone, believe it or not. My sister gave it to me. But I sometimes forget to charge it." He tore a piece of paper from the edge of a magazine and started writing. "My wife always wanted me to get one, but…" He lifted the pencil, showed a blank stare, and finished writing. "Anyway, give this to your boyfriend. Tell him to call me, and I'll pay him to help me fix my truck."

"He's not my…" Kay shook her head and stuck the paper in her pocket. "OK. Sure. I'll give this to Matt."

Calder followed the girls to the porch and pointed to a well-worn path leading into the woods. "If you don't mind walking your bikes a ways, that's a shortcut to Swamp Road. It goes through Wilbour Woods. It'll be dark soon and this will save you a few minutes."

"Let's take the path. Then I know we can get back to the house before Mom."

"I don't know." Anna's eyes widened. "What if it's really dark in there."

"This is not like a scene from a horror movie," Kay said. "This is quiet, laid-back Little Compton. Let's get going."

"It's easy," Calder said. "I take my walks through there all the time. Your bikes'll make it."

Kay grabbed the handlebars. "Let's go." Twenty yards down the path, she stopped.

"What's the matter?"

"Nothing. I need to blow my nose."

Anna walked up beside Kay. "You're crying."

"I wanted to help Elena, and I failed."

"You didn't fail," Anna said. "I know you wanted to help, and you tried your hardest."

Kay twisted around. In the dim light, the woods seemed to close behind her like a big, green elevator door. "We'd better get moving."

Five minutes into the walk, Anna stopped and grabbed Kay's arm. "This path splits off in two directions. Which way should we go?"

"I say we go right."

Anna pointed. "But I think I heard a car in that direction."

"I didn't hear anything." Kay pulled a coin from her pocket. "Call it. Heads we go your way; tails we go mine." She flipped the coin and slapped it against the back of her hand. "Tails." The two pushed off into the dark woods.

"Kay, wait." Anna checked her watch. "It's been ten minutes since we took your path, and I still don't see the road. And it's getting darker. Are you sure this is the way?"

"Positive." Kay's eyes scanned left and right, straining to see the path ahead. "I think cars have driven through here."

Anna took in a quick breath. "What was that sound?"

"What sound? I didn't hear anything."

A long, high-pitched howl echoed through the woods.

Kay walked her bike a few feet and stood close to Anna. "Now I hear it. Maybe it's a coyote."

"What? Coyotes? In Rhode Island?"

"Elena said they've migrated from out West. She had a dozen chickens at one time, and the coyotes killed most of them."

Anna's hands shook so much on the handlebars that the bike chain rattled. "Will they attack us?"

"Elena said coyotes don't attack humans."

Dark figures, distorted by the outline of the trees, moved parallel to the bikers' path.

"What's that?" Anna rotated her head left and right.

"I don't know," Kay said, "and I don't want to find out. Let's go."

Anna screamed. "Look out!"

The shadowy figures leaped from the tree line, almost brushing Kay's front tire. She flinched, letting her bike tilt to one side and almost falling into the bushes.

"It was a deer," Kay said, swallowing hard. "Two of them—maybe the mama and her baby. They scared me, too."

Her hands trembling, Anna grabbed Kay's arm.

"It's OK. The deer won't hurt us." She pulled away from Anna's grip. "My phone's ringing." She snatched the vibrating phone from her pocket. "Oh, no. It's Mom."

Twenty yards from the girls, a pair of bright lights bounced up and down in the darkness. The lights stopped moving, and a single intense light jerked its beam in several directions, finally focusing on Kay and Anna.

"The light's coming toward us," Anna said. "What's happening?"

CHAPTER FORTY-FIVE

"Thanks again, officer." Bobbie let the door slam shut and walked inside. "You didn't leave me a note. I went to see Elena, thinking you girls might be over at the cottage. Then I saw your bikes were gone. I was very worried."

Kay swallowed a mouthful of water and set the glass on the counter. "How did the police know we were in Wilbour Woods?"

"I saw a map by the computer. It had this Mr. Calder's address on it and Matt's name. I called Matt and he said maybe you had gone to see Mr. Calder. I gave the police Calder's address."

Kay pulled her bottom lip over her top. "I'm sorry, Mom. I...we didn't mean to make you worry."

"Kay, you'll soon be fifteen. You need to be more responsible."

"I said I'm sorry. It's just that..." Small tears trickled down Kay's cheeks. "Mom, I went to see Mr. Calder. He's the man I told you about—the one that Matt and I talked to. I wanted so much to help Elena, but nothing I tried helped the situation. Elena might have to sell Windcrest, or she'll have to work full time and leave Zack home alone."

Bobbie put her arm around Kay. "I'm sorry, dear." She moved back to stand squarely in front of her daughter, both her hands on Kay's shoulders. "You did the best you could."

"Maybe I didn't do enough. I let Elena down."

"You didn't let her down." Bobbie wiped a tear from Kay's face. "Don't say that."

"The houses will be built, and the view from Windcrest Farm will be tacky fences and the backs of houses, and nobody but us will want to stay here. Plus, Hank's dad lost his job, and his family will move away, and Anna won't ever see Hank, and Elena will have to get another job, and...and..."

Bobbie and Anna led Kay to the sofa and sat beside her.

Kay's mom grabbed a tissue from the box on the end table and gave it to her daughter. "You're not responsible for any of that."

Anna pulled out her phone. "It's a message from Hank. He says his dad got a job offer from an engineering company in Providence."

Kay sat forward, sniffing and grabbing another tissue. "Really? That's great news."

Bobbie stroked Kay's hair and gave her a peck on the cheek. "Try to forget all this and enjoy the rest of the time we have here at Windcrest."

Kay took both hands and brushed away the tears. "OK. I'll try. I mean, I will."

"Go lie down for a while. Anna can help me with dinner. We'll call you when it's ready."

Kay closed the door and fell across the bed, burying her head in the pillow to muffle the sound of her sobbing.

CHAPTER FORTY-SIX

"The cookout was a great idea," Kay said. "We cleaned the place up pretty good after the hurricane."

Bobbie set a dish of sliced tomatoes on the table. "I wanted to end our stay on a high note."

Kay looked at Anna. "Having you and Matt here makes it that much more special for me, and it made this vacation one of the best ever. But it would've been even better if I could have helped Elena and Zack."

"You should be very proud of what you tried to do for them," Bobbie said. "But, sometimes things don't always work out the way you want them to."

"Funny you should say that. Dad sent me an e-mail with the serenity prayer."

Anna tapped her friend on the elbow. "What's a serenity prayer?"

"Let me see if I can recite it: 'God, grant me the serenity to accept the things I cannot change, the courage to change the things I can, and the wisdom to know the difference.'" Kay nodded at her mom. "I'm gradually learning the difference."

Elena helped Zack get his chair over a clump of grass in the lawn behind the cottage and rolled over to the two large folding tables. "We're here."

Zack lifted a large dish from his lap. "And here's Zack's specialty—vegetable lasagna made with Elena's famous zucchini."

"I wish my husband had a specialty," Bobbie said. "Even one that's not so special. Cook *something*."

Elena showed a sympathetic frown—a frown combined with a smile. "That's not fair. Jim's not here to defend himself."

"I'd cook a lot more," Zack said. "But, to be honest, our kitchen isn't set up for a chef in a wheelchair. My wife is my sous chef."

Kay stood next to Zack. "Any time I'm up here in Little Compton, I'll be your sous chef." She turned around at the sound of a car engine. "Who's that?"

"It's Hank and his mom and dad." Anna walked toward the car.

Kay's face lost its color.

"We thought it would be nice to invite the McCallums." Bobbie walked up behind her daughter. "Elena met Mr. McCallum a few days ago for lunch."

Kay whipped around. "Why didn't you tell me?"

"We were afraid you'd stress too much."

"You're right. I would have. And I'm stressing now. They're coming over."

Kay gave a small hand wave. "Hi, Hank. How's the head?"

"Better, thanks," he said, touching his forehead. The boy cleared his throat and reached out for Kay's hand, drawing her close. "Dad, you remember Kay."

"Yes, I do. We met a few weeks ago."

Kay extended her trembling hand, her face red like the farm-fresh sliced tomatoes in the dish on the table. "I apologize if I was a little rude when you came to the door before."

McCallum shook her hand and wrapped his other hand on top, followed by a warm smile. "You don't have to apologize for anything."

"Thank you." Kay's voice cracked. "But I am sorry you lost your job."

McCallum put on that fatherly smile, the one dads give daughters to say everything's all right. "The only thing you did was help me make my decision. In a way, I owe you."

"I'm glad you feel that way, and that something good happened for you."

Elena moved next to Kay. "Excuse, me, Henry. I want you to meet Zack. You come, too, Kay."

Elena introduced Kris and Henry McCallum.

"Great to meet you, Zack." McCallum extended his hand. "And thank you for your service to our country."

Zack smiled. "I'm happy to meet you, sir. Thank you for saying that."

"I understand the house and the cottage are not exactly easy to get around in," McCallum said.

"We manage, but it can be a little frustrating."

Elena chimed in. "A lot frustrating."

"OK. The narrow doors and counters that I can't reach do make life a little difficult." He slapped the tops of his thighs. "But I've been in worse situations."

"Those situations are well behind you," McCallum said, staring at the empty footplates. "But I'd like to do something about the one you're in now."

Zack looked at McCallum, and jerked his head toward Elena and then back.

"For the past few years, I've been on the board of a foundation that helps wounded veterans," McCallum said. "This week I applied for a grant to get money to do some changes to the cottage and the house. I want to make it user friendly to veterans like you and to any disabled person who might come to Windcrest Farm."

Zack swallowed hard, grabbed Elena's hand, squeezing tight, and looked up at McCallum. "Thank you. I don't know what to say."

"You don't have to say anything."

"*I* have to say something." Elena gave the man a hug. "Thank you."

Tears trickled down Kay's face. "I'll let you guys talk, and I'll take Hank over to Matt and Anna."

Sitting next to Kay, Matt raised himself off the bench three times and craned his neck to see over Hank and Anna, sitting on the opposite side of the table.

On Matt's fourth attempt to see something beyond the picnic table, Kay strained to see across the table in the same direction. "Is something wrong?"

"No. Nothing's wrong. I was just...nothing, really."

Five minutes later, the sound of crunching gravel in the driveway caught everyone's attention.

"I've seen that pickup." Kay moved to her right the same time Anna moved to her left to turn around. "Anna, I can't see." She rose off the bench a few inches. "It's Mr. Calder." Kay jerked her head in Matt's direction. "What's going on?"

Matt avoided eye contact, slid out of the bench, and walked over to the truck. He escorted Sam Calder to the table.

"Hi, Mr. Calder," Kay said, casting a quick and puzzled glance at Matt. "It's nice to see you again."

Calder winked. "Same here, young lady."

Matt introduced the man to the only people who had not met him, the McCallums, Kay's mom, and Zack Clifford.

"We have something in common." Calder shook Zack's hand and held it for a good fifteen seconds. "You and I need to talk."

Zack pivoted his chair around and stared at his wife.

"Matt and Kay told me about Mr. Calder," Elena said, leaning close to her husband. "I called him and asked him if he would talk to you."

Zack's gaze darted from Calder, back to his wife, and then to Kay.

"Mr. Calder lost his legs in Vietnam," Kay said. "He's the one who owned the land where the new houses are going up."

"Thanks, Kay, but you got part of that wrong." Calder winked at Matt. "I *own* the land—or *will own it* soon, anyway."

"Wait a minute." Kay looked around the table. All eyes were on her, and every face had either a knowing smile or a wide grin. "Am I the only one who didn't know this?"

Bobbie and Elena rose and stood behind Kay.

"Matt went to see Mr. Calder a few days ago," Elena said. "He helped him fix his truck."

"I'm a pretty good mechanic," Matt said. "I learned a lot keeping my old pickup patched together." He moved over and let Calder slide onto the bench next to Kay.

"While we worked on my truck, Matt and I chatted. He convinced me that my dear wife would have wanted me to do something to help keep that land as beautiful as it is now. Didn't take much convincing to get the owner to sell." Calder put on the winner's smile—a smile that comes with a nod and a wink. "Money talks real loud."

Kay beamed from ear to ear. "What are you going to do with the land?"

"I'm putting it in the conservancy. Can't be used for anything but farming. That's what my wife would have wanted." He held Kay's hand. "She was a lot like you. You're quite a remarkable young lady. Your boyfriend Matt told me about you."

Her eyes wide, Kay looked at Matt, saw him staring back, and quickly looked away.

"Yep, working with the FBI and almost falling off that bridge, that's something out of a movie." Calder shook his head. "And scuba diving for gold with Matt—now, that's one story to tell your kids some day."

Kay's mouth was cotton dry. Boyfriend. Kids. Gold. What had Matt been telling him?

"Gold? What gold?" Bobbie pivoted away from Calder, looking back and forth at Matt and Kay.

In seconds, Kay went from total embarrassment at the boyfriend reference to wondering if she'd be grounded till she went to college. She closed her eyes. Why did this have to come out now.

"Yes, sir, that diving for gold in Maine would make a best seller," Calder said. "Somebody should write a book about this girl."

Kay opened her eyes. Thoughts of her parents finding out about Maine raced through her mind. And a book? The whole world would know.

Bobbie touched her daughter's shoulder. "Kay?"

Kay turned and gave her mom a hug, trying to put on a smile that didn't quite break through. "Yes, ma'am?" The teen was never disrespectful to her mom, but she only used the word "ma'am" when she was deep in trouble. With a sheepish grin, she pulled back from her mom and looked at Anna and Matt. Both had eyes wide and mouths open.

Bobbie asked again. "Is there something you need to tell me?"

Kay started to speak, her voice squeaky and high-pitched. She cleared her throat and drew her shoulders up. "Maybe."

THE END

About the Author

Sonny Barber developed an interest in American history at an early age, reading and collecting newspapers, magazines, and other materials on historic US and world events. He has coupled that interest with his fiction writing to create a modern-day "mystery history" series for preteens and older readers. Sonny graduated from Georgia State University with a degree in journalism. His work as a writer, editor, and photographer has taken him across the United States and to many other countries. He and his wife live in South Florida. Their two daughters have provided some of the inspiration for the teenaged characters in his books.

30821309R00094

Made in the USA
Middletown, DE
08 April 2016